Justin Huntly McCarthy

Marjorie

Justin Huntly McCarthy

Marjorie

1st Edition | ISBN: 978-3-75243-655-6

Place of Publication: Frankfurt am Main, Germany

Year of Publication: 2020

Outlook Verlag GmbH, Germany.

MARJORIE

BY

Justin Huntly McCarthy

CHAPTER I

MY APOLOGY

What I have written may seem to some, who have never tossed an hour on salt water, nor, indeed, tramped far afield on dry land, to be astounding, and well-nigh beyond belief. But it is all true none the less, though I found it easier to live through than to set down. I believe that nothing is harder than to tell a plain tale plainly and with precision. Twenty times since I began this narrative I have damned ink and paper heartily after the swearing fashion of the sea, and have wished myself back again in my perils rather than have to write about them.

I was born in Sendennis, in Sussex, and my earliest memories are full of the sound and colour and smell of the sea. It was above all things my parents' wish that I should live a landsman's life. But I was mad for the sea from the first days that I can call to mind.

My parents were people of substance in a way—did well with a mercer's shop in the Main Street, and were much looked up to by their neighbours. My mother always would have it that I came through my father of gentle lineage. Indeed, the name I bore, the name of Crowninshield, was not the kind of name that one associates usually with a mercer's business and with the path in life along which my father and mother walked with content. There certainly had been old families of Crowninshields in Sussex and elsewhere, and some of them had bustled in the big wars. There may be plenty of Crowninshields still left for aught I know or care, for I never troubled my head much about my possible ancestors who carried on a field gules an Eastern crown or. I may confess, however, that in later years, when my fortune had bettered, I assumed those armes parlantes, if only as a brave device wherewith to seal a letter. Anyway, Crowninshield is my name, with Raphael prefixed, a name my mother fell upon in conning her Bible for a holiname for me. So, if my arms are but canting heraldry, I carry the name of an archangel to better them.

I was an only son, and my parents spoilt me. They had some fancy in their heads that I was a weakling, and needed care, though I had the strength of a colt and the health a sea-coast lad should have, so they did not send me to a school. Yet, because they set a store by book-learning—which may have its uses, though it never charmed me—I had some schooling at home in reading, writing, and ciphering. My father sought to instil into me an admiration for the dignity of trade, because he wished me to become a merchant in time, with mayhap the Mayoralty in perspective. I liked the shop when I was little, and thought it a famous place to play in, lurking down behind its dark counter as in a robbers' den, and seeing through the open door of the parlour at the back of the shop my mother knitting at her window and the green trees of the garden. I liked, too, the folds of sober cloth and coloured prints, and the faces of folk when they came in to buy or cheapen. Even the jangle of the bell that clattered at the shop door when we put it to at meal times pleased my ears, and has sounded there many times since and softly in places thousands of miles away from the Main Street. I do not know how or why, but the cling-clang of that bell always stirred strange fancies in my mind, and strange things appeared quite possible. Whenever the bell went tinkle I began to wonder who it was outside, and whether by chance they wanted me, and what they might want of me. But the caller was never better than some neighbour, who needed a button or a needle.

The great event of my childhood was my father's gift to me of an English version of Monsieur Galland's book, 'The Arabian Nights' Entertainments.' Then the tinkle of the shop bell assumed a new significance. Might not Haroun al Raschid himself, with Giafar, his vizier, and Mesrour, his man, follow its cracked summons, or some terrible withered creature whom I, and I only, knew to be a genie in disguise, come in to catch me by the shoulder and sink with me through the floor?

Those were delicious terrors. But what I most learnt from that book was an unconquerable love for travel and an unconquerable stretching to the sea. When I read in my book of Sinbad and his Seven Voyages I would think of the sea that lay so near me, and wish that I were waiting for a wind in a boat with painted hull and sails like snow and my name somewhere in great gold letters. I would wander down to the quays and watch the shipping and the seamen, and wonder whence they came and where they went, and if any one of them had a roc's egg on board. I was very free for a child in those days, for my parents, still fretting on my delicacy, rarely crossed me; and, indeed, I was tame enough, partly from keeping such quiet, and well content to be by myself for the hour together.

But, when I had lived in this wise until I was nearly fifteen, my father and my mother agreed that I needed more book-learning; and, since they were still loath to send me to school, they thought of Mr. Davies, the bookseller, of Cliff Street. He was a man of learning. His business was steady. He had leisure, and was never pressed for a penny, or even for a guinea. It was agreed that I should go every day for a couple of afternoon hours, to sit with him and ply my book, and become a famous scholar. Poor Mr. Davies! he never got his will of me in that way, and yet he bore me no grudge, though it filled him with disappointment at first.

3

There was a vast deal of importance for me, though I did not dream it at the time, about my going to take my lessons of Mr. Davies, of Cliff Street. For if I had not gone I should never have got that tincture of Latin which still clings to me, and which a world of winds and waters has not blown or washed from my wits; nor, which is far more important, should I ever have chanced upon Lancelot Amber; and if I had not chanced upon Lancelot Amber I should have lost the best friend man ever had in this world, and missed seeing the world's fairest woman.

CHAPTER II

LANCELOT AMBER

Mr. Davies was a wisp of a man, with a taste for snuff and for snuff-coloured garments, and for books in snuffy bindings. His book-shop in Cliff Street was a dingy place enough, with a smell of leather and paste about it, and if you stirred a book you brought enough snuffy dust into the air to make you sneeze for ten minutes. But his own room, which was above the shop, was blithe enough, and it was there I had my lessons. Mr. Davies kept a piping bullfinch in it, and a linnet, and there was a little window garden on the sill, where tulips bloomed in their season, and under a glass case there was a plaster model of the Arch of Titus in Rome, of which he was exceedingly proud, and which I thought very pretty, and at one time longed to have.

Mr. Davies was a smooth and decent scholar, and when he was dreamy he would shove his scratch back from his forehead and shut his eyes and recite Homer or Virgil by the page together, while Lancelot and I listened open-mouthed, and I wondered what pleasure he got out of all that rigmarole. The heroes of Homer and of Virgil seemed to me very bloodless, boneless creatures after my kings and wizards out of Mr. Galland's book; even Ulysses, who was a thrifty, shifty fellow enough, with some touch of the sea-captain in him, was not a patch upon my hero, Sindbad of Bagdad, from whose tale I believe the Greek fellow stole half his fancies, and those the better half.

I remember still clearly the very first afternoon when I presented myself at Mr. Davies's shop in Cliff Street. He told me I was very welcome, assured me that on that day I crossed the threshold of the Muses' Temple, shook me warmly by the hand, and then, all of a sudden, as if recollecting himself, told me to greet my class-fellow. A lad of about mine own age came from the window and held out his hand, and the lad was Lancelot Amber.

I have seen many gracious sights in my time, but only one so gracious as that sudden flash of Lancelot Amber upon my boyish vision. As he came forward with the afternoon sunlight strong upon him he looked like some militant saint. There is a St. George in our church, and there is a St. Michael too, both splendid in coat-armour and terrible with swords, but neither of them has ever seemed to me half so heroic or half so saintly as the boy Lancelot did that morning in Mr. Davies's parlour. He was tall of his years, with fair hair curling about his head as I have since seen hair curling in some of the old Pagan statue-work.

The boy came forward and shook hands with me in friendly fashion, with a friend's grip of the fingers. I gave him the squeeze again, and we both stood for a moment looking at each other silently, as dogs over-eye one another on a first meeting. How little it entered into either of our brains that moment of the times that we should stand together, and the places and the trials and perils that we should endure together. We were only two lads standing there in a snug first-floor room, where yellow parrots sprawled on the painted wall, and a mild-mannered gentleman with a russet wig motioned us to sit down.

Our life ran in current for long enough. We sat together at Mr. Davies's feet—I am speaking metaphorically, for in reality we sat opposite to him—and we thumbed our Cordery and our Nepos together, and made such progress as our natures and our application permitted. Mine, to be honest, was little enough, for I hated my grammar cordially.

Lancelot was not like me in this, any more than in bodily favour; he was keen of wit and quick of memory; he was quick in learning, yet as modest as he was clever, for he never sought in any way to lord it over me because I, poor dunce, was not of such nimble parts as himself.

It was the hardest task in the world for me to keep my eyes and my fancy upon the pages of my book. My eyes were always straying from the print, first to the painted parrots on the walls, and then, by natural succession, to the window. Once there, my fancy would put on free wings, and my thoughts would stray joyously off among the salt marshes, where the pools shone in the sunlight and a sweet air blew. Or I would stand upon the downs and look along the curve of cliffs, and note the ships sailing round the promontory, and the flashes of the sea beyond, and feel in fancy the breeze blowing through my hair, and puffing away all the nonsense I had been poring over in the room.

At such times I would quite forget myself, and sit staring into vacancy, till Mr. Davies, lifting his nose from his volume, would note my absence and call on me by name, and thump his desk, and startle me with some question on the matter we were supposed to have in hand. A mighty matter, truly, the name of some emperor or the date of some campaign—matter infinitely less real than the name of the ship that was leaving the harbour or the sunlight on the incoming sail. And I would answer at random and amiss, and earn reproof. Yet there were things which I knew well enough, too, and could have given him shrewd and precise answers concerning them.

Lancelot Amber was never much my companion away from Mr. Davies's room. His father, whose name he perpetuated, had been a simple, gentle gentleman and scholar who had married, as one of his kin counted it, beneath him, because he had married the woman he loved. The woman he loved was indeed of humble birth, but she made him a fair wife and a good, and she bore him two children, boy Lancelot and girl Marjorie, and died for the life of the lass. Her death, so I learned, was the doom of Lancelot Amber the elder, and there were two babes left in the wood of the world, with, like the children in the ballad, such claims upon two uncles as blood might urge and pity supplement. These two uncles, as Lancelot imagined them to me, were men of vastly different stuff and spirit, as you may sometimes find such flaming contrasts in families. The elder, Marmaduke Amber, used the sea, and was, it seems, as fine a florid piece of sea flesh as an island's king could wish to welcome. His brother, Nathaniel, had been a city merchant, piling up moneys in the Levant trade, and now lived in a fine house out in the swelling country beyond Sendennis, with a fine sea-view. Him I had seen once or twice; a lean monkey creature with a wrinkled walnut of a face and bright, unkind eyes. He was all for leaving the boy of three and the girl of two to the small mercies of some charity school, but the mariner brother gathered the two forlornlings to his great heart, and with him they had lived and thriven ever since. Now it seems Captain Marmaduke was on a voyage to the Bermudas and taking the maid with him, while the boy, to better his schooling and strengthen his body with sea air, was sent to Sendennis to stay with his other uncle, Nathaniel Amber, now, to all appearance, reconciled to the existence of his young relative. This uncle, as I gathered, did not at first approve overmuch of Lancelot taking lessons in common with a single mercer's son, but Mr. Davies, I believe, spoke so well of me that the arrangement was allowed to hold.

But after lesson hours were done Lancelot had always to go back to his uncle's, and though I walked part of the way, or all the way, with him most days of the week, I was never bidden inside those doors. Lancelot told me that he had more than once besought leave to bring me in, but that the old gentleman was obdurate. So, save in those hours of study in the parrot-papered room, I saw but little of Lancelot.

I never expected to be asked inside the doors of the great house where Lancelot's days were passed, and I did not feel any injustice in the matter. I was only a mercer's son, while Lancelot derived of gentlefolk, and it never entered into my mind to question the existing order of things, or to wish to force my way into places where I was not wanted. Excellent gentlemen on the other side of the Atlantic have made very different opinions popular from the opinions that prevailed with me in my youth. Indeed, I myself have now been long used to associate with the great folk of the earth, and have found them in all essential matters very much like other men. I have had the honour of including more than one king amongst my acquaintances, and have liked some and not liked others, just as if they were plain Tom or Harry. But in the days of my youth I should have as soon expected to be welcomed at St. James's as to be welcomed in the great house where Lancelot's uncle lived.

———————————————————————————

CHAPTER III

THE ALEHOUSE BY THE RIVER.

Three years after I went to learn under Mr. Davies, of Cliff Street, my father died.

I remember with a kind of terror still, through all these years, when death of every kind has been so familiar to me, how the news of that death came upon me. I had no realisation of what death meant till then. I had heard of people dying, of course; had watched the black processions creeping, plumed and solemn, along the streets to the churchyard; had noted how in any circle of friends now one and now another falls away and returns to earth. I knew that all must die, that I must die myself, as I knew a lesson got by heart which has little meaning to the unawakened ear. But now it came on me with such a stabbing knowledge that for a little while I was almost crazy with the grief and the fear.

But the sorrow, like all sorrows, lessened with time. There was my mother to cheer; there was my schooling to keep; there was the shop to look after.

My father had thriven well enough to lay by a small store, but my mother kept the shop on, partly for the sake of my father, whose pride it was, partly because it gave her something to occupy her widowed life, and partly because, as Mr. Davies pointed out to her, there would be a business all ready for me when I was old enough to step into it. In the meantime my life was simple enough. When I was not taking my schooling with Lancelot I was tending the shop with mother; and when I was doing neither of these things I was free to wander about the town much as I pleased.

Our town was of a tidy size, running well back from the sea up a gentle and uneven acclivity, which made all the streets that stemmed from the border slightly steep, and some of them exceedingly so. Upon the coast line, naturally enough, lay the busiest part of the hive; a comely stretch of ample docks and decent wharves along the frontage of the town, and, straggling out along the horns of the harbour, a maze of poorer streets, fringed at the waterside with boozing-kens, low inns, sailors' lodging-houses, and crimperies of all kinds. There were ticklish places for decent folk to be found in lying to right and left of the solemn old town—aye, and within ten minutes' walk of the solemn old market-square, where the effigy of Sir William Wallet, the goodly and godly Mayor of many years back, smiled upon the stalls of the hucksters and the fine front of the town-hall. If you strayed but a little way from the core of the town you came into narrow, kinkled streets, where nets were stretched across from window to window drying; and if you persevered you came, by cobbly declivities, to the bay shore, and to all the odd places that lay along it, and all the odd people that dwelt therein.

Of course, with the inevitable perversity of boyhood, it was this degenerate quarter of the town which delighted me. I cared nothing, I am sorry to say, for the fine-fronted town-hall, nor for the solemn effigy of Sir William Wallet. I had not the least desire ever to be a functionary of importance in the building, ever to earn the smug immortality of such a statue. I am sorry to say the places I cared for were those same low-lived, straggling, squalid, dangerous regions which hung at one end of respectable little Sendennis like dirty lace upon a demure petticoat. In the early days of my acquaintance with those regions I must confess that I entered them with a certain degree of fear and trembling; but after a while that feeling soon wore off, when I found that no one wanted to do me any harm. Indeed, the dwellers in those parts were generally too much occupied in drinking themselves drunk and sleeping themselves sober to note an unremarkable lad like me. As for their holiday time, they passed it so largely in quarrelling savagely, and occasionally murderously, amongst themselves that they had scant leisure to pay any heed to me. For the rest, these Sendennis slums were not conspicuously evil. You will find just the same places in any seaport town, great or little, in the kingdom. But there was one spot in Sendennis which I do not think that it would be easy to match in any other town, although, perhaps to say this may be but a flash of provincial pride on my part.

A good way from the town, and yet before the river fairly widens into an estuary, there stood a certain hostel, or inn, which it was my joy and my sorrow to haunt. It stood by the water's edge in a kind of little garden of its own; a dreary place, where a few sickly plants tried to hold their own against neglect and the splashings of rinsed glasses. There was a wooden terrace at the back of this place—the back overlooked the river, while the front was on the by-road—and here the habitual revellers, the haunters, whose scored crosses lent the creaking shutters an unnatural whiteness over their weather-beaten surface, dark with age and dirt, loved to linger of a summer evening, and ply the noggin and fill the pipe.

There was an old fiddler, a kind of Orpheus of the slums, who would sometimes creep in there and take his post in a corner and begin to play, happy if the mad lads threw him halfpence, or thrust a half-drained tankard under his tearful old nose: happy, too, if they did not—as they often did—toss the cannikin at him out of mere lightness of heart and drunkenness of wit. He used to play the quaintest old tunes, odd border-side ballad airs, that seemed to go apace with blithe country weddings and decent pastoral merry-makings of all kinds, and to be strangely out of suits with that brotherhood of rakehells, smugglers, and desperadoes who gambled and drank, and swore and quarrelled, while the poor old fellow worked his catgut.

Lord, Lord, how the memory of it all comes back upon me while I write! I have but to close my eyes, and my fancy brings me back to that alehouse by the river, to a summer's eve with its golden shafts falling on the dingy woodwork and lending it a pathetic glory, upon the shining space of dwindled water in the middle of its banks of glistening mud, and there in the corner the pinched old rogue in his ragged bodygear scraping away at 'Barbara Allen,' or 'When first I saw thy face,' or 'The Bailiff's Daughter of Islington,' while the leering rascals in the pilot coats and the flap-eared caps huddled together over their filthy tables, and swigged their strong drink and thumbed their greasy cards and swore horribly in all the lingoes of Babel.

One such summer evening surges up before me with a crimson smear across its sunlight. There was a Low Country fellow there, waist deep in schnapps, and a Finlander sucking strong beer like a hog. Meinheer and the Finn came to words and blows, and I, who was sitting astride of the railing staring, heard a shrill scream from the old man and a rattle as he dropped his fiddle, and then a flash and a red rain of blood on the table as my Finn fell with a knife in him, the Hollander's knife, smartly pegged in between the left breast and the shoulder. I declare that, even in my excitement at that first sight of blood drawn in feud, my boyish thought was half divided between the drunken quarrel and the poor old fiddler, all hunched together on the ground and sobbing dry-eyed in a kind of ecstasy of fear and horror. I heard afterwards that he had a son knifed to his death in a seaman's brawl, and never got over it. As for the Finn, they took him home and kept it dark, and he recovered, and may be living yet for all I know to the contrary, and a perfect pattern to the folk in Finland.

That inn had a name, stranger I have never heard; and a sign, stranger I have never seen; though I have wandered far and seen more than old Ulysses in the school-book ever dreamt of. It was called the Skull and Spectacles; and if its name was at once horrible and laughable, its sign was more devilish still. For instead of any painted board, swinging pleasantly on fair days and creaking lustily on foul, there stood out over the inn door a kind of bracket, and on that bracket stood a human skull, so parched and darkened by wind and weather that it looked more fearful than even a *caput mortuum* has a right to look.

On the nose of this grisly reminder of our mortality some wag—or so I suppose, but perhaps he was a cynic—had stuck a great pair of glassless barnacles or goggles. It was a loathly conceit, and yet it added vastly to the favour of the inn in the minds of those wildings that haunted it. Must I add that it did so in mine too, who should have known better? If it had not been for the fascination of that sign, perhaps I might have kept better company, and never done what I did do, and never written this history.

When first I happened upon the Skull and Spectacles it attracted me at once. Its situation, in the middle of that wilderness of mouldering wharves, decaying gardens, and tumble-down cottages, was in itself an invitation to the eye. Then the devilish mockery of its sign was an allurement. It looked like some fantastical tavern in a dream, and not a thing of real timber.

The oddness of the place tickled my adventurous palate, the loathsomeness of the sign gripped me hardly by the heart and made my blood run icily for an instant. Who does not recall to mind moments and places when he seems to have stepped out of the real living world into some grey, uncanny land of dreams, where the very air is thick and haunted with some quality of unknown fear and unknown oppression? So it seemed to me when I first saw the Skull and Spectacles with its death's-head smirking welcome and the river mud oozing about its timbers. But the place piqued me while it frightened me, and I pulled my courage together like a coat, buttoned it metaphorically about me, and entered.

Like many another enterprise upon which we enter with a beating heart, the preface was infinitely more alarming than the succeeding matter. There was no one in the bar-parlour when I entered save a sailor, who was sleeping a drunken, stertorous sleep in a corner. From the private parlour beyond, when I entered, a man came out, a burly seafaring man, who asked me shortly, but not uncivilly, what I wanted. I called for a jug of ale. He brought it to me without a word, together with a hunch of bread, set them before me, and left me alone again, going into his snuggery at the back, and drawing the door after him jealously.

I sat there for some little time, sipping my ale and munching my bread—and indeed the ale was excellent; I have never tasted better—and looking at the grimy wall, greasy with the rubbings of many heads and shoulders, scrawled all over with sums, whose addition seemed to have mightily perplexed the taproom arithmeticians, and defiled with inscriptions of a foul, loose-witted, waterside lubricity that made me blush and feel qualmish. But I found a furtive enjoyment in the odd place, and the snoring sailor, and the low plashing of the estuary against the decaying timbers, and the silence of solitude all around.

Presently the door was pushed open; but before anyone could come in I was made to jump from my seat in a kind of terror, for a voice sang out sharply just above my head and startled me prodigiously.

'Kiss me—kiss me—kiss me—kiss me!' the strange voice screamed out. 'Kiss me on the lips and eyes and throat! kiss me on the breast! kiss me—kiss me—kiss me!'

I turned up my eyes and noted above my head what I had not seen before—a cage swinging from the rafters, and in it a small green parrot, with fiery eyes that glowed like blazing rubies.

It went rattling on at an amazing rate, adjuring its hearers to kiss it on all parts of the body with a verbal frankness that was appalling, and with a distinctness which even pricked the misty senses of the slumberer, who peevishly turned in his sleep and stuttered out a curse at me to keep still.

As the human voice called me back from my contemplation of that infernal old bird my lowered eyes looked on the doorway. The door was wide open, and a girl stood framed in the gap, gazing at me. Lord, how the blood rushed into my face with wonder and delight, for I thought then that I had never seen anything before so beautiful! Indeed, I think now that of that kind of beauty she was as perfect as a woman could wish to be, or a man could wish to have her. She smiled a little into my crimson, spell-bound face, wished me good-morning pleasantly, gave a kind of little whistle of recognition to the bird, who never left off screaming and yelling his vociferous desire for kisses, and then, swinging the door behind her, crossed the floor, and, passing into the parlour, disappeared from my gaze.

Immediately the parrot's clamour came to a dead pause. The semi-wakened sailor dropped into his sodden snooze again, and all was quiet. I waited for some little time with my eyes on the parlour door, but it did not open again; and as no one came in from outside, and I needed no more either of drink or victual, I felt that I must needs be trudging. So I drained my can to the black eyes of my beauty, clucked at the parrot, who merely swung one crimson eye round as if he were taking aim and glared ferociously, signed a farewell to the parlour door, and passed out into the world again. The Skull and Spectacles had gained a devoted customer.

Ah, me! I went there a world of times after that. I am afraid my poor mother thought me a sad rogue, for I would slip away from the shop for a whole afternoon together, on the plea of needing a walk; but my walk always led me to that terrible inn. I soon became a familiar figure to its ill-favoured master and his beautiful niece. The landlord of the Skull and Spectacles had been a seaman in his youth, and told tales of the sea to guests who paid their score. He had a cadet brother who was a seaman still, and who drifted out of longshore knowledge for great gaps of time, and came back again liker to mahogany than he had been before, a thought more abundant in blasphemy, and a great deal richer in gold pieces with the heads of every king in

Christendom stamped upon them.

It was this wanderer's daughter who made the place my paradise. She was a tall, largely made girl, of a dark favour, with eyes of black fire, and with a warm, Spanish kind of skin, olive-toned with rich reds under, and the whitest, wonderfullest teeth, and a bush of black hair that was a marvel. She would let it down often enough, and it hung about her body till it reached the back of her knees. Lord knows who her mother was. I never knew, and she said she never knew. Her father brought her home much as he had brought the parrot home, but I could never think other than that she was the child of some Spanish woman he had wooed, and, it is to be hoped, wedded, though I doubt if he were of that temper, on his travels in the South Americas.

A very curious thing it was to watch that girl go in and out among the scoundrelly patrons of the Skull and Spectacles, listening to their devil's chatter in all the lingoes of earth, and yet in a kind of fashion keeping them at a distance. She would bandy jokes with them of the coarsest kind, and yet there was not a man of all the following who would dare to lay a rude hand on her or even to force a kiss from her against her will. Every man who clinked his can at that hostelry knew well enough that her father, when he was ashore, or her uncle, when the other was afloat, would think nothing of knifing any man who insulted her.

I need hardly say that my association with the Skull and Spectacles greatly increased in me my longing for the adventurous life. The men who frequented the inn had one and all the most marvellous tales to tell. Their tales were not always commendable; they were tales of pirates, of buccaneers, of fortunes made in evil wise and spent in evil fashion. But it was not so much the particulars as the generalities of their talk that delighted me. I loved to hear of islands where the cocoa trees grew, and where parrots of every hue under heaven squealed and screamed in the tropic heat; where girls as graceful as goddesses and as yellow as guineas wore robes of flaming feathers and sang lullabies in soft, impossible tongues; lands of coral and ivory and all the glories of the earth, where life was full of golden possibilities and a world away from the drab respectability of a mercer's life in grey Sendennis.

I grew hungrier and thirstier for travel day after day. I had heard of seamen in a shipwrecked craft suffering agonies of thirst and being taunted by the fields of water all about them, to drink of which was madness and death. I felt somewhat as if I were in like case, for there I lived always in the neighbourhood, always in the companionship of the sea and of seafaring folk, and yet I was doomed to dwell at home and dance attendance upon the tinkling of the shop bell. But my word was my word all the same, and my love for my mother, I am glad to think, was greater after all than my longing to see far lands.

_____

15

CHAPTER IV

A MAID CALLED BARBARA

I suppose the Skull and Spectacles was not quite the best place in the world for a lad of my age, and perhaps for some lads it might have been fruitful of evil. But I found then, and have found all through my life, an infinite deal of entertainment in studying the ways and humours of all kinds of fellowships, without of necessity accommodating myself to the morals or the manners of the company. I have been very happy with gipsies on a common, though I never poisoned a pig or coped a nag. I have mixed much with sailors of all kinds, than whom no better fellows—the best of them, and that is the greater part—exist on earth, and no worse the worse; and yet I think I have not been stained with all the soils of the sea. I have been with pirates, and thieves, and soldiers of fortune, and gentlemen of blood, and highway robbers; and once I supped with a hangman—off boiled rabbit and tripe, an excellent alliance in a dish—and all this without being myself either pirate, highwayman, or yet hangman. It is not always a man's company, but mostly a man's mind, that makes him what he is or is not. If a man is going to be a pitiful fellow and sorry knave, I am afraid you will not save him by the companionship of a synod of bishops; nor will you spoil a fine fellow if he occasionally rubs shoulders with rogues and vagabonds.

The girl at the Skull and Spectacles was kind to me, partly, perhaps, because I differed somewhat from the ordinary ruck of customers of the Skull and Spectacles. Had it been known that that crazy, villainous old alehouse contained such a pearl, I make no doubt that the favour of the place would have gone up, and its customers improved in outward seeming, if not in inward merits or morals. The gallants of the town—for we had our gallants even in that tranquil seaport—would have been assailed by a thirst that naught save Nantz and schnapps and strong ale of the Skull and Spectacles could assuage, and the gentlemen of the Chisholm Hunt would have discovered that the only way after a run with the harriers was through the vilest part of the town and among the oozy timbers of the wharves which formed the kingdom of the Skull and Spectacles.

"She Had Always a Pleasant Smile for Me When I Came."

But few of the townspeople knew of the Skull and Spectacles. It never thought to stretch its custom into the higher walks of life. It throve on its own clients, its high-booted, thick-bearded, shaggy-coated seamen, whose dealings with the sea were more in the way of smuggling, buccaneering, scuttling, and marooning than in honest merchandise or the service of the King. These sea-wolves liked the place famously, and would have grievously resented the intrusion of the laced waistcoats of the provincial dandies or the scarlet jackets of the Chisholm Hunt. So the Skull and Spectacles went its own way, and a very queer way, too, unheeded and unheeding.

How the girl and I got to be so friendly I scarcely know. It is like enough that I thought we were more friendly than we really were, and that the girl took my boyish homage with more indifference than I guessed for. She had always a pleasant smile for me when I came, and she was always ready to pass a pleasant word or two with me, even on the days when the business in the place was at its heaviest, and when the room was choking fit to burst with the shag-haired sea-fellows.

But there were times, too, better times for me, or worse, it may be, when the Skull and Spectacles was almost deserted; when all its wonted customers were away smuggling, or buccaneering, or cutting throats, or crimping, or following whatever was their special occupation in life.

In such lonely times the girl was willing enough to spend half an hour or more in speech with me. Of course, I fell in love with her, like the donkey that I was, and worshipped the rotting boards of the Skull and Spectacles because she was pleased to walk upon them. Her speech was all of strange lands, and it fed my frenzy as dry wood feeds a fire. Her people were all sea-people, her talk was all sea-talk, her words were all sea-words. It was a strange rapture to me to sit and listen while she spoke of the things that were dearest to my heart and to watch her while she spoke. Then I used to feel a wild, foolish longing, which I had never the courage to carry out, to tell her how beautiful she was —as if she needed to be told that by me!—and how madly I loved her. All of which I very profoundly thought and believed, but all of which—for I was a shy lad with women-kind—I kept very devoutly to myself.

I wonder if the girl had any idea of my devotion. I thought she had; I felt sure that my love must be as patent to her as it was to myself, and that she must needs prize it a little. I believe, indeed, that I never talked to her very much during those happy times when she would come out on to the creaking terrace and speak to me of the things which she never seemed to weary of—the sea, and ships, and seamen. As for me, who would not have wearied of any theme that gave her pleasure, had it even been books and lessons, I was overjoyed that my sea longings could help me on with her.

Then her black eyes would follow the river's course to where the estuary widened to the sea, and search the horizon and point out to me the sails that starred it here and there, and sometimes say with a laugh: 'Perhaps one of those is my ship.'

But when I asked her what was her ship she would smile and shake her head and say nothing; and once, when I asked her if it was her father's ship, she laughed loudly and said yes, it was her father's ship she longed for.

So late spring slipped into early summer; and, as the year grew kinder, so every day my boy's heart grew hotter with its first foolish passion. Somewhere about the middle of June, as I knew, her birthday was; and in view of that saint's day of my calendar I had hoarded my poor pocket money to buy her a little toy from the jeweller in the Main Street, whose show seemed to me more opulent than the treasures of Aladdin.

The day found me all of a tremble. I had sat up half the night looking at my token and kissing it a thousand times. It was a little locket that was fashioned like a heart, and on the one side her name was engraved, and on the other mine, for I thought by this to show what I dared not say.

It was early when I stole from our shop, little less than ten, and I calculated that I would look in at Mr. Davies's on my way back and make some excuse for my truancy, and so be back in time for noonday dinner; and I knew if I were a little late my mother would forgive me. Lord, how I ran along the quays! I seemed to fly, and yet the road seemed endless. As I ran I noted that some new ships had entered the night before, and men on the wharves were busy unloading, and sailors were lounging round with that foreign air which Jack always has after a cruise.

When I got to the Skull and Spectacles the landlord was standing before his door smoking. As he saw me he nodded, and when I asked for Barbara, saying I had a message for her, he told me she was upstairs, and added something which I did not stay to hear.

I bounded up the crazy stairs with a beating heart. I was all on fire with excitement at the thought of offering her a gift; my blood seemed to be turned to quicksilver, and to race through its channels with a feverish swiftness.

There was a gallery at the head of the stairs, a gallery on to which looked the doors of the guest-rooms of the inn—rooms where bearded men from over sea sometimes passed a night when they were uncertain where to journey next, or when they were too much pleased with the liquor of the Skull and Spectacles to leave it before morning.

As I swung round the stairs into the gallery I thought for a moment that it was empty, as it lay before me dark and uninviting. Then from the far end came the sound of voices, laughter, and laughing expostulation—this last in a woman's voice that I knew too well. While I stood staring, not understanding, and bewildered by a sudden and wholly meaningless alarm, one of the doors at the end of the gallery that was just ajar swung open, and Barbara slipped from it, laughing, breathless, with tumbled hair and crimson cheeks. A man sprang after her and caught her, unreluctant, in his arms.

I see the scene now as vividly as I saw it then with my despairing boyish eyes. The great strong man had his arms close about her; her dark hair was all about her face and over her shoulders as she flung her head back to meet the great red mouth that was seeking hers. I have seen since pictures of satyrs embracing nymphs, and whenever I see them I cannot stay a shudder running through me as I think of that dim, creaking gallery and the dishevelled girl and the strong man and the tearful, trembling lad who beheld their passion.

I suppose a painter would have admired the group they made; she with her body eagerly flung forward and her beautiful face all on fire with warm animal emotion; he, big and amber-bearded, his great mouth crushed against hers as if he wanted to absorb her life, and his arms about her pliant body, at once yielding and resisting in its reckless disarray. But I was not a painter— only a longshore mooncalf—and my eyes swam and my tongue swelled till I thought it would stick between my teeth as those of poor rogues do on the gallows, and I was chickenish enough to wish to blubber. And while I stood there, stockish and stupid, the pair became aware of me. I do not think I made any noise, but their eyes dropped from each other and turned on me, and the man scowled a little, without loosening his hold, but the woman, no whit troubled, flung one arm away from her lover's neck and held out her hand to me, with a laugh, and greeted me merrily.

'Why, it's little Raphael!' she said, laughing the words into the yellow beard of the sea-thief who clipped her, and again she nodded at me, in no ways discomposed by the strangeness of her position. But I, poor fool, could not bear it, and I turned and ran down the stairs as if the Devil himself were after me.

CHAPTER V

LANCELOT LEAVES

There was a place upon the downs to which it was often my special delight to betake me—a kind of hollow dip between two humps of hills, where a lad might lie warm in the windiest weather and look straight out upon the sea, shining with calm or shaggy with storm, and feel quite as if he were alone in the world. To this place I now sped half unconsciously, my face, I make no doubt, scarlet with passion and shame, and my eyes well-nigh blinded with sudden up-springing of tears. How I got to my hollow I do not know, but I ran and ran and ran, with my blood tingling, heedless of all the world, until at last I found myself tumbling down over its ridged wall or rampart of hummocks and dropping, with a choking moan, flat on my face in an agony of despair.

There I lay in the long grasses, sobbing as if my heart would break. Indeed, I thought that it was breaking; that life was over for me; that sunrise and sunset and the glory of the stars had no further part to play for me; and that all that was left for me was to die, and be put into a corner somewhere and speedily forgotten.

Troops of bitter thoughts came surging up over my brain. My mood of mind and state of body were alike incomprehensible and terrible to me. It was a very real agony, that fierce awakening to the realities of life, to love and passion, and blinding jealousy and despair, and all the rest of the torments that walk in the train of a boy's first love. I wallowed there a long time, making a great mark in the soft grasses, as if I sought to measure myself for an untimely grave. The strong afternoon sun drove on his way westward, and still I lay there, writhing and whimpering, and wondering, perhaps, a little inwardly that the sky did not fall in and crush me and the wicked world altogether.

A boy's mind is a turbulent place enough, and stuffed pretty often with a legion of wicked thoughts, which take possession of his fancy long before evil words and evil deeds have struck up their alliance. Yet even the most foul-mouthed boy thinks, I believe, nobly, or with a kind of nobility, of his first love, and a clean-hearted lad offers her a kind of bewildering worship. I was a clean-hearted lad, and I had worshipped Barbara; and now my worship was over and done with, and I made sure that my heart was broken.

I do not know how long I lay there, with whirling brain and bursting heart, but presently I felt the touch of a hand on my shoulder. I had heard no one

21

coming, and under ordinary conditions I might have been a thought startled by the unexpected companionship; but just now I was too wretched for any other emotion, and I merely lay passive and indifferent.

The hand declined with a firmer pressure and gently shook my shoulder, and then a voice—Lancelot Amber's voice—called softly to me asking me what I was doing there and what ailed me. I always loved Lancelot's voice: it seemed to vary as swiftly as wind over water with every thought, and to run along all the chords of speech with the perfection of music in a dream. Whenever I read that saying of St. Paul's about the tongue of men and of angels I am reminded of Lancelot's voice, and I feel convinced that of such is the language of the courts of heaven, and that if St. Paul had talked like Lancelot he would have won the most sceptical. The sound of his voice soothed me then, as far as it was possible for anything to soothe me, and I shifted slightly to one side and looked up at him furtively and crossly, my poor face all blubbered with tears and smeared with mire where I had lain grovelling.

Bit by bit I told him my story. I was in the temper for a confession, and ready to tell my tale to anyone with wit enough to coax it from me. Perhaps it did not seem so much of a tale in the telling, though to my mind it was then as terrible as the end of the world itself and the unloosening of the great deep.

So I hunched myself up on my left elbow, and, staring drearily at Lancelot through my tears, I whimpered out my sorrows; and he listened with a smileless face.

When I had done, and my quavering broke off with a sob, he was silent for a while, looking straight before him beyond the meadow edges into the yellowing sky. Then he turned and looked at me with a brotherly pity that was soothing to my troubled senses, and he spoke to me with a softness of voice that seemed in tune with the dying day and my drooping spirits.

'After all,' he said, 'you have not lost much, Raphael. She is but a light o' love, and you were built for a better mate.'

Truly, though I scarcely noted it at the time, it was gracious and quick-witted of him to assume that I was of a lover's age with the great lass of the Skull and Spectacles, and unconsciously it tickled my torn vanity. But part of his speech angered me, and I took fire like tinder.

Swinging myself round on my elbow, I glanced savagely into Lancelot's face of compassion.

'You lie!' I growled, 'you lie! She is a queen among women, and there is no man in all the world worthy of her!'

22

Then—for I saw him smile a little—I struck out at him. I am thankful to think that I was too wild and weary to strike either true or hard, and my foolish hand just grazed his cheek and touched his shoulder as he stooped; and then, turning away again, I fell into a fresh storm of sobbing. Lancelot remained by my side, gently indifferent to my fury, gently tender with my sorrow. After a while he turned me round reluctant, and looked very gravely into my tear-stained face. We were but a brace of lads, each on the edge of life, and as I look back on that page of my history I cannot help but shudder at the contrast between us, I bellowing like a gaby at the ache of my first calf-love—and yet indeed I was hurt, and hardly—and he so sweet and restrained and sane, weighing the world so wisely in his young hands.

'I am very sorry for you, Raphael,' he said, and his voice was so clear and strong that for the moment it comforted me as a cordial will comfort a sick man, against my will. 'I am very sorry for you, and because of my sorrow for you and because of my love for you I will give you a gift that I would part with to no other in the world. Women are not all alike, and therefore I will give you a talisman to help you to think well of women.'

I suppose it would have diverted an elder to hear him, so slim and simple, discoursing so sweetly and reasonably on a theme on which few of us at the fag end of our days are ever able to utter one sensible syllable, but Lancelot always seemed to me wise beyond his time, so I listened, although dully enough and I fear sullenly. He slipped his hand into his breast and drew forth a small object which he held shut in his hand while he again discoursed to me.

'What I am going to give you, Raphael, is the little picture of a lass who is in my eyes a thing of Heaven's best making. For loyalty, honour, courage, truth, faith, she is an unmatchable maid. I have known her all the days of my life and never found a flaw in her.'

Then he opened his hand and I saw that it held a picture, an oval miniature in a fine gold frame. My mind was all on fire for the black eyes of piratical Barbara and my blood was tingling to a gipsy tune, but as I stared at the image in my comrade's palm my mind was arrested and my fancy for the instant fixed. For it showed the face of a girl, a child of Lancelot's age or a little under, and through my tears I could perceive the sweetness of the countenance and its likeness to my friend in the fair hair and the fine eyes.

'This is my sister, this is Marjorie,' Lancelot said slowly. 'She has the truest soul, the noblest heart in all the world. I think it will help you to have it and to look on it from time to time, as it always helps me when I am away from her.'

As he spoke he pushed the picture gently into my unresisting fingers and closed them over it. 'My sister Marjorie is a wonderful girl,' he said, with a bright smile. He was silent for a little while as if musing upon her and then his tender thoughts returned to me.

'Come away, Raphael,' he said. 'Let us be going home. The hour is late, and your mother may be anxious; and you have her still, whatever else you may have lost.'

The grace of his voice conquered me. I rose at the word, staggering a little as I gained my feet, for passion and grief had torn me like devils, and I was faint and bewildered. He slipped his arm into mine and led me away, supporting me as carefully as if I were a woman whom his solicitude was aiding. We exchanged no word together as we went along the downs and through the fields. As we came to the town, however, he paused by the last stile and spoke to me.

'Dear heart!' he said, 'but I am sorry for all this—more sorry than I can say; for I am going away to-morrow.'

The words shook me from myself and my apathy. I gazed in wonder and alarm into his face.

'I am going away,' he said, 'and that's how I chanced to find you. For I waited in vain for you at Mr. Davies's, and sought you at your home and found you missing; and then I thought of this old burrow of yours, and here, as good luck would have it, I found you.'

I could only gasp out 'Going away?' in a great amazement.

'I must go away,' he said. 'My uncle that was at sea is in London, with Marjorie, and has sent for me. He needs me, and I am so much beholden to him that I should have to go, even if I were not bound to him by blood and duty, and indeed I long to see my Marjorie.'

'How long will you be away?' I gasped.

'I do not know,' he answered; 'but it is only a little world after all, and we shall meet again some time, and soon, be sure of that. If not, why, then this parting was well made.'

This last was a quotation from one of his poets and play-makers, as I found afterwards, for the words stuck in my memory, and I happened on them later in a printed book. But indeed I did not think the parting was well made at all, and I shook my head dismally, for I knew he only said so to cheer me.

He laughed and tossed his brown locks. 'London is not the end of the world,' he said. 'I hope to go further afield than that before I die. But near or far, summer or winter, town or country, we are friends for ever. No distance can divide, no time untie our friendship.'

Here he wrung me by the hand, and I, with this new sorrow on top of the old
—that was new but two hours ago—could only sob and say: 'O Lancelot!'
and tremble. I suppose I looked giddy, as if I were about to faint, for he
caught me in his strong arms and propped me up a minute.

'Come, come!' he said; 'take heart. To-day is not to-morrow yet. I will go in
with you to your mother's and spend an hour with you before I say good-bye.'

Then he gently led me by the arm, and we went into the town and along the
evening streets till we came to the little shop, and there at the door we found
my mother, looking anxious.

Lancelot made my excuses, saying that he had kept me, and telling my mother
of his speedy departure. My mother, who loved Lancelot, was almost as
grieved as I. But he, in his bright way, cheered us; he came in, and would take
supper with us; and though it was a doleful meal, he went on as if it were a
merry one, talking and laughing, and telling us tales of the great city and its
wonders, and all he hoped to see and do there.

And so a sad hour went by, and then he rose and said he must go and give a
hand to the packing of his belongings, for he was leaving by the early coach
and would not have a moment in the morning. And then he kissed my mother
and kissed me, and went away and left us both crying. There were tears in his
own eyes as he stepped out into the summer twilight, but he turned to look
back at us, and waved his hat and called out good-bye with a firm voice.

A sullen blackness settled down upon me after Lancelot's departure. I was
minded to rise early in the morning to see him off by the coach, but I was so
tired with crying and complaining that when I fell asleep I slept like a log, and
did not wake until the morning sun was high and the coach had been long
gone. Well, it was all the better, I told myself savagely. He had gone out of
my life for good, and I should see no more of him. I had lost in the same hour
my love and my friend. I would make up my mind to be lonely and pay no
heed. As for the picture he gave me, what good to me was the face of that fair
girl? Lancelot's sister Marjorie was a gentlewoman, born and bred, as my lost
Lancelot was a gentleman. What could she or he really have to do with the
mercerman in the dull little Sussex town? Marjorie had a beautiful face, if the
limner did not lie—and indeed he did not—and I could well believe that as
lovely a soul as Lancelot lauded shone through those candid eyes. But again,
what was it to me and my yardwand? So I hid the picture away in a little
sweet-scented cedar-wood box that I had, and resolved to forget Lancelot and
Lancelot's sister, and everything else in the world except my blighted youth
and my blighted hopes.

I reasoned as a boy reasons who thinks that the world has come to an end for him after his first check, and who has no knowledge as yet of the medicine of time. My mother had but a vexatious life of it with me, for I was silent and melancholy; and though I never, indeed, offended her by uncivil word or deed, yet the sight of my dreary visage must have been a sore trial to her, and the glum despondency with which I accepted all her efforts to cheer me from my humours must have wrung her heart.

Poor dear! She thought, I believe, that it was only grief for Lancelot which touched me so; and once, after some days of my ill-temper, she asked me if I would like to run up to London and see my friend. But I shook my head. I had made up my mind to have done with everything; to stay on there to the end, morosely resigned to my lot.

To make myself more sure in isolation I even took the letter which came from Lancelot but a few days after his departure, in which he told me where his uncle's house was, and bade me write to him there, and burnt it in the flame of a candle. As I tossed the charred paper out into the street I thought to myself that now indeed I was alone and free to be miserable in my own way. And I was miserable, and made my poor mother miserable; and acted like the selfish dog I was, like the selfish dog that every lad is under the venom of a first love-pang.

I went no more to the Skull and Spectacles; I saw my beautiful tyrant no more. One day I drifted along in the familiar direction, came to the point where I could see the evil-favoured inn standing alone in the dreary waste, hesitated for a moment, and then, as the image of the girl in the sailor's arms surged up before my mind, I turned and ran back as hard as I could into the town.

But if I went that way no more, I drifted about in other ways helplessly and foolishly enough.

I would spend hours upon hours mooning among the downs and on the cliffs, and sometimes I would sit on some bulkhead by the quays and look at the big ships, and wish myself on board one of them and sailing into the sunset. Love for my mother kept me from going to the devil, but my love for her was not strong enough to put a brave face upon my trouble, and I was not man enough to do my best to make her life light for her.

But no trouble of this kind does endure for ever, and by the end of a year the poison had in a great degree spent itself, and with my recovery from my love-ache there grew up in my mind a disdain of my behaviour. As I saw my mother's visage peaked with pity I grew to be heartily ashamed of myself, and to resolve honestly and earnestly to make amends. I disliked tending shop more bitterly than ever. But there was the shop, and it was dear to my mother's heart; and so I buckled to, if not with a will, at least with the semblance of a will, and did my best to become as good a mercer as another.

Two things, however, I would not do. I would not enter into correspondence with Lancelot, and I would not go any more to Master Davies's house. Lancelot wrote again and yet again to me. But I served the second letter as I had served the first, and the third as I had served the second. I did, indeed, scrawl some few lines of reply to this last letter, bidding him somewhat bluntly to leave me in peace; that my bed had been made for me, and that I must needs lie upon it, and that I did not wish to be vexed in my slumber. It was a rude and foolish letter, I make no doubt; but I wrote it with a decent purpose enough, for I was desperately afraid that I could not hold to my resolutions and to my way of life if I kept in communication with Lancelot, and was haunted by the thoughts of his more fortunate stars. Lancelot wrote back to me with his invariable sweetness and gentleness, saying that he hoped time would make me amends; and after that I heard no more from him, and he seemed to have passed out of my life for good and all.

As for Mr. Davies, he too seemed to belong to the old life from which I had cut myself adrift, and so I went to his shop no more; and as he was a home-keeping bookworm, he but seldom stirred abroad. And thus, though we dwelt in the same town, I may fairly say that I never saw him from month's end to month's end.

The days slip by swiftly in an unnoticeable kind of way in a town like Sendennis. It was but a sluggish place, for all its sea-bustle, in the days that now lie far behind me. Our shop lay in the quietest part of the town, and we took no note of time. Ours was a grey, lonely life. We had friends, of course, whose names and ways I have long since forgotten, but we saw little of them, partly because my mother learnt after a while that I hated all company, and would take no part in any of the junketings of our neighbours.

I might have made an apt mercer in time, but I do not know, and I do not love to linger over the two years I spent in the trial. For though I did my duty fairly well, both by my mother and by the shop, and though my love-ache had dulled almost to nothing, my passion to go abroad was as hot as ever, and I thought it a shame that my twenty years had no better business, and my life no other aim, than to wear out its strength behind a counter. Let those two years go by.

One evening I was sitting with my mother in the little parlour behind the shop, she knitting, I think, or sewing—I am not sure which—and I with my legs thrust out before me and my hands in my pockets, outwardly idling and inwardly cursing at my destiny. Every now and then my mother glanced at me over the edge of her work and sighed; but it may have been, and I hope it was, because she found her task a difficult one.

Suddenly the bell at the front door tinkled. In my younger days I used to fancy that every ring of that same cracked bell brought some message from the outer world for me. Well, here was the message at last, though I never dreamt of it, but just sat stupidly, with my fingers touching my pocket seams.

CHAPTER VI

THE GENTLEMAN IN BLUE

My mother glanced up from her work at me. I knew that her look asked me if I had heard the bell, and if I would not go to the door in answer; and, though I felt lazy, I was not base enough to ignore that appeal. So I lurched up from my chair and swung through the little shop and flung the door wide open, a thought angrily, for I had been deep in my brown study and was stupidly irritated at being jarred from it.

I half expected, so far as I expected anything, to see some familiar neighbour, with the familiar demand for a twist of tape or a case of needles, so that I confess to being not a little surprised and even startled by what my eyes did rest upon. The doorway framed a wholesome picture of a middle-aged comely gentleman.

I see the stranger now in my mind's eye as I saw him then with my bodily vision—a stoutly made, well set-up man of a trifle above the middle height, in a full-skirted blue coat; a gold-laced hat upon his powder, and a gold-headed cane in his hand. The florid face was friendly, and shrewd too, lined all over its freshness with little lines of experience and wisdom and knowledge of the world, and two honest blue eyes shone straight at me from beneath bold black eyebrows.

It was certainly a most unfamiliar figure in the framework of our shop door, and I stood and stared at it, somewhat unmannerly, for a space of several seconds. After a while, finding that I still barred his way and said nothing, the stranger smiled very good-humouredly; and as he smiled I saw that his teeth were large and white and sound.

'Well, young sir,' he said pleasantly, 'are you Master Raphael Crowninshield?'

I told him that was my name.

'Then I should like to exchange a word or two with you,' he said; 'can we be private within?'

I answered him that there was no one inside but my mother, and I begged him to step into the little parlour.

The stout gentleman nodded. 'Your mother?' he said. 'Very good; I shall be delighted to have the honour of making madam's acquaintance: bring me to her.'

I led the way across the shop and up the two low steps into the little parlour, where my mother, who had heard every word of this dialogue, had laid aside her sewing, and now rose as the stranger approached and dropped him a curtsey.

'Be seated, madam, I beg,' said the stranger. 'I have a word or two to say to your son hereby, but first'—here he paused and addressed himself to me —'prithee, lad, step to the door a moment and wait till I call for you. Your mother and I have our gossip to get over.'

There was something so commanding in the kindliness of the stranger's manner and voice that I made no hesitation about obeying him; so I promptly rose and made for the shop, drawing close the door of the parlour behind me.

I stood awhile at the outer door, looking listlessly into the street, and wondering what the blue gentleman could have to say to my mother and to me. Even now I can recall the whole scene distinctly, the windy High Street, with its gleams of broken sunlight on the drying cobbles—for it had rained a little about noon, and the black clouds were only now sailing away towards the west and leaving blue and white sky behind them. I can see again the signs and names of the shops opposite, can even recall noting a girl leaning out of a window and a birdcage in an attic.

When the door of the parlour behind me opened for the blue-coated gentleman I noted that my mother stood with a pale face and her hands folded. He beckoned me to him and clapped his hand on my shoulder, and though he laid it there gentle enough, I felt that it could be as heavy as the paw of a bear.

'My lad,' he said, gazing steadily into my face with his china-blue eyes, 'your good mother and I have been talking over some plans of mine, and I think I have induced her to see the advantage of my proposals. Am I right or am I wrong in assuming you have stowed away in your body a certain longing for the wide world?'

I suppose my eyes brightened before my lips moved, for he cut me short with: 'There, that's all right; never waste a word when a wink will do. Now, am I right or am I wrong in supposing that you have a good friend whose name is Lancelot Amber?'

I was determined that I would speak this time, and I almost shouted in my eagerness to say 'Yes.'

'That will be a good voice in a hurricane,' the blue gentleman said approvingly. Then he began again, with the same formula, which I suppose pleased his palate.

'Am I right or am I wrong in assuming that he has told you of a certain old sea-dog of an uncle of his whose name is Marmaduke Amber?'

I nodded energetically, for after his comment I thought it best to hold my tongue.

'Very good. Now, am I right or am I wrong in supposing that you feel pretty sure at this moment that you are looking upon that same old sea-dog, Marmaduke Amber?'

This time I smiled in good earnest at his fantastic fashion of self-introduction, observing which the blue gentleman swayed me backwards and forwards several times with his right hand, and I felt that if I had been an oak of the forest he would have swayed me just as easily, while he said with a kind of approbative chuckle: 'That's right—a very good lad; that's right—a very smart lad.' Then he suddenly lifted his hand, and I, unprepared for the removal of my prop, staggered against the counter, while he put another question.

'And what do you think Marmaduke Amber wants with you?'

I shook my head, and said I could not guess.

'Why, to make a man of you, to be sure,' the gentleman answered. 'You are spoiling here in this hen-coop. Now, Lancelot loves you like a brother, and I love Lancelot like a father, and I am quite prepared to take you to my heart for Lancelot's sake, for he is scarce likely to be deceived in you. You must know that I am going to embark upon a certain enterprise—of which more hereafter. Now, the long and the short of it is that Lancelot is coming with me, and he wants to know, and I want to know, if you will come too?'

'If I would come too!'

My heart seemed to stand still for joy at the very thought. Why, here was the chance I was longing for, dreaming of, day and night; here was a great ship waiting to carry me on that wrinkled highway of my boyish ambition; here was the change from the little life of a little town into the great perils and brave existence of the sea; here was a good-bye to love and sorrow, and the putting on of manhood and manly purposes!

Would I not come! My lips trembled with delight and my speech faltered, and then I glanced at my mother. She was very pale and sad, and at the sight my joy turned to sorrow. She saw the change on my face, and she said, very quietly and resolutely: 'I have given my consent, my dear son, to your going hence. Perhaps it is for the best.'

'Mother,' I said, turning towards her with a choking voice, 'indeed—indeed it is for the best. I should only mope here and fret, and come to no good, and give you no pride in me at all. I must go away; it will not be for long; and when I come back I shall have forgotten my follies and learnt wisdom.' Lord, how easy we think it in our youth to learn wisdom! 'And you will be proud to see me, and love me better than ever, for I shall deserve it better.'

Then my mother wrung her hands together and sighed, and tried to speak, but she could not; and she turned away from us and moved further back into the room. I made a step forward, but the stranger caught me by the shoulder, and swinging me round, guided me to the door; and at the door we stood in silence together for some seconds, staring out into the street.

'Have patience, lad,' he whispered into my ear; 'it is a good woman's weakness, and it will pass soon. She knows and I know that it is best for you to go.'

I could say nothing, for my heart was too full with the joy of going and with grief for my mother's grief. But I felt in my soul that I must go, or else I should never come to any good in this world, which, after all, would break my mother's heart more surely and sadly.

Presently we heard her voice, a little trembling, call on Mr. Amber by his name, and we went slowly back together. Already, as I stood by that stalwart gentleman and timed my step to his stride, I began to feel as if I had known him all my life, and had loved him as we love some dear kin.

I do not know how I can quite express what I then felt, and felt ever after, in his company—a kind of exultation, such as martial music stirs in any manly bosom, or as we draw in from the breath of some brave ballad. It would be impossible, surely, to feel aught but courageous in such cheerful, valiant, self-reliant fellowship.

CHAPTER VII

CAPTAIN MARMADUKE'S PLAN

Seated in the back parlour, with his chair tilted slightly back, Captain Marmaduke Amber set forth his scheme to us—perhaps I should say to me, for my mother had heard it all, or most of it, already, and paid, I fancy, but little heed to its repetition. For all the attention I paid, I gained, I fear me, but a very vague idea of Captain Marmaduke's purpose. I was far too excited to think of anything clearly beyond the fact that I was actually going a-travelling, and that the jovial gentleman with the ruddy face and the china-blue eyes was my good angel. Still, I gathered that Captain Amber would be a colonist—a gentleman-adventurer; after a new fashion, and not for his own ends.

It was, indeed, a kind of Utopia which Captain Amber dreamt of founding in a far corner of the world, beneath the Southern Cross. The Captain had taken it into his gallant head that the old world was growing too small and its ways too evil for its people, and that much might be done in the way of the regeneration of human society under softer surroundings and beneath purer skies. His hope, his belief, was that if a colony of earnest human beings were to be founded, established upon true principles of justice and of virtue, it might set an example which would spread and spread until at last it should regenerate the earth.

It was a noble scheme indeed, prompted by a kindly and honourable nature, and I must say that it sounded very well as the periods swelled from Captain Amber's lips. For Captain Amber was a scholar and a gentleman as well as a man of action, and he spoke and wrote with a certain florid grace that suited him well, and that impressed me at the time very profoundly. It seemed to me that Captain Amber was not merely one of the noblest of men—which indeed he was, as I was to learn often and often afterwards—but also one of the wisest, and that his scheme of colonisation was the scheme of a statesman and a philosopher.

How precisely the thing was to be done, and why Captain Marmaduke seemed so confident of finding a new Garden of Eden or Earthly Paradise at the other end of the world, I did not rightly comprehend then; nor, indeed, have I striven much to comprehend since. But I gathered this much—that Captain Marmaduke had retired from the service to carry out his fancy; that he had bought land of the Dutch in the Indies; that he had plenty of money at his command; and that the enterprise was all at his charges. One thing was quite certain—Captain Marmaduke had got a ship, and a good one too, now riding at anchor in Sendennis harbour; and in Sendennis Captain Marmaduke only meant to stay long enough to get together a few more folk to complete his company and his colony. I was to come along, not as a colonist, unless I chose, but as a kind of companion to Lancelot, to learn all the tricks of the sailor's trade, and to return when Captain Marmaduke, having fairly established his colony, set out on his return voyage.

For it seemed that if I had forgotten, or seemed to have forgotten, Lancelot, he had not forgotten me, but had carried me in his thoughts through all the months that had grown to years since last we met. Thus, when Captain Amber first began to carry out his dream of a colony, Lancelot begged him to give me a share in the adventure. For Lancelot remembered well my hunger and thirst for travel, and had sworn to help me to my heart's desire. And it seemed to him that in this enterprise of his uncle's lurked my chance of seeing a little of the world.

Captain Amber, who loved Lancelot better than any being in the world save one, promised that if I were willing, and seemed a lad of spirit, I should go along with Lancelot and himself to help build the colony at the butt end of the world. As the ship was to sail from Sendennis—that being Captain Amber's native place—he promised Lancelot that he would seek me out, and see if I pleased him, and if the plan pleased me. And I, on fire with the thought of getting away from Sendennis and feeling the width of the world—all I wanted to know was how soon we might be starting.

'A fortnight is our longest delay,' the Captain said; 'we sail sooner if we can. Report yourself to me to-morrow morning between eleven and noon. You will find me at the Noble Rose. You know where that is, I suppose?'

Now, as the Noble Rose was the first inn in Sendennis, and one that the town was proud of, I naturally knew of its whereabouts, though I was not so well acquainted with it as with a certain other and more ill-favoured hostelry that shall be nameless. The Noble Rose was in favour with the country gentry and the gentlemen of the Chisholm Hunt, and it would scarcely have welcomed a tradesman's son within its walls as readily as the rapscallion Skull and Spectacles did. But I felt that I should be welcomed anywhere as the friend of Captain Marmaduke Amber, for as a friend I already began to regard him. So I assured him that I would duly present myself to him at the Noble Rose on the morrow, between eleven of the clock and noon.

'That's right, lad,' he said; and then, turning to my mother, he took her worn hand in his strong one, and, to my surprise and pleasure, kissed it with a reverential courtesy, as if she had been a Court lady.

As Captain Marmaduke turned to go I caught at his hand.

'Where is Lancelot?' I asked; 'is he here in Sendennis?' For in the midst of all the joy and wonder of this sea business my heart was on fire to see that face again.

Captain Marmaduke laughed.

'If he were in Sendennis at this hour he would be here, I make no doubt. He is in London, looking after one or two matters which methought he could manage better than I could. But he will be here in good time, and it is time for me to be off. Remember, my lad, to-morrow,' and with a bow for my mother and a bear's grip for me he passed outside the shop, leaving my mother and me staring at each other in great amazement. But for all my amazement the main thought in my mind was of a certain picture of a girl's face that lay, shrined in a cedar-wood box, hidden away in my room upstairs. And so it happened that though my lips were busy with the name of Lancelot my brain was busy with the name of Marjorie.

CHAPTER VIII

THE COMPANY AT THE NOBLE ROSE

The next morning I was up betimes; indeed, I do not think that I slept very much that night, and such sleep as I did have was of a disturbed sort, peopled with wild sea-dreams of all kinds. In my impatience it seemed to me as if the time would never come for me to keep my appointment with Captain Marmaduke; but then, as ever, the hands of the clock went round their appointed circle, and at half-past eleven I was at my destination. The Noble Rose stood in the market square. It was a fine place enough, or seemed so to my eyes then, with its pillared portal and its great bow-windows at each side, where the gentlemen of quality loved to sit of fine evenings drinking their ale or their brandy, and watching the world go by.

In the left-hand window as I came up I saw that the Captain was sitting, and as I came up he saw me and beckoned me to come inside.

With a beating heart I entered the inn hall, and was making for the Captain's room when a servant barred my way.

'Now then, where are you posting to?' he asked, with an insolent good-humour. 'This is a private room, and holds private company.'

'I know that,' I answered, 'but it holds a friend of mine, whom I want to see and who wants to see me.'

The man laughed rudely. 'Very likely,' he said, 'that the company in the Dolphin are friends of yours,' and then, as I was still pressing forward, he put out his hand as if to stay me.

This angered me; and taking the knave by the collar, I swung him aside so briskly that he went staggering across the hall and brought up ruefully humped against a settle. Before he could come at me again the door of the Dolphin opened, and Captain Marmaduke appeared upon the threshold. He looked in some astonishment from the rogue scowling on the settle to me flushed with anger.

'Heyday, lad,' he said, 'are you having a bout of fisticuffs to keep your hand in?'

'This fellow,' I said, 'tried to hinder me from entering yonder room, and I did but push him aside out of my path.'

'Hum!' said Captain Marmaduke, ''twas a lusty push, and cleared your course, certainly. Well, well, I like you the better, lad, for not being lightly balked in your business.' And therewith he led me into the Dolphin.

There was a sea-coal fire in the grate, for the day was raw and the glow welcome. Beside the fire an elderly gentleman sat in an arm-chair. He had a black silk skull-cap on his head, and his face was wrinkled and his eyes were bright, and his face, now turned upon me, showed harsh. I knew of course that he was Lancelot's other uncle, he who would never suffer that I should set foot within his gates. Indeed, his face in many points resembled that of his brother—as much as an ugly face can resemble a fair one. There was a likeness in the forehead and there was a likeness in the eyes, which were something of the same china-blue colour, though of a lighter shade, and with only cold unkindness there instead of the genial kindness of the Captain's.

A man stood on the other side of the open fireplace, a man of about forty-five, of something over the middle height and marvellously well-built. He was clad in what, though it was not distinctly a seaman's habit, yet suggested the ways of the sea, and there was a kind of foppishness about his rig which set me wondering, for I was used to a slovenly squalor or a slovenly bravery in the sailors I knew most of. He was a handsome fellow, with dark curling hair and dark eyes, and a dark skin that seemed Italian.

I have heard men say that there is no art to read the mind's complexion in the face. These fellows pretend that your villain is often smooth-faced as well as smooth-tongued, and pleases the eye to the benefit of his mischievous ends. Whereas, on the other hand, many an honest fellow is damned for a scoundrel because with the nature of an angel he has the mask of a fiend. In which two fancies I have no belief. A rogue is a rogue all the world over, and flies his flag in his face for those who can read the bunting. He may flatter the light eye or the cold eye, but the warm gaze will find some lurking line by the lip, some wryness of feature, some twist of the devil's fingers in his face, to betray him. And as for an honest man looking like a rogue, the thing is impossible. I have seen no small matter of marvels in my time—even, as I think, the great sea serpent himself, though this is not the time and place to record it—but I have never seen the marvel of a good man with a bad man's face, and it was my first and last impression that the face of Cornelys Jensen was the face of a rogue.

CHAPTER IX

THE TALK IN THE DOLPHIN

Captain Marmaduke presented me to the two men, while his hand still rested on my shoulder.

'Brother,' he said, 'this is Master Ralph Crowninshield, of whom you have often heard from Lancelot.'

'Aye,' said the old man, looking at me without any salutation. 'Aye, I have heard of him from Lancelot.'

Captain Marmaduke now turned towards the other man, who had never taken his eyes off me since I entered the room.

'Cornelys Jensen, here is Master Ralph Crowninshield, your shipmate that is to be.'

Cornelys Jensen came across the room in a couple of swinging strides and held out his hand to me. Something in his carriage reminded me of certain play-actors who had come to the town once. This man carried himself like a stage king. We clasped hands, and he spoke.

'Salutation, shipmate.'

Then we unclasped, and he returned to his post by the fireplace with the same exaggeration of action as before.

The old man broke a short silence. 'Well, Marmaduke, why have you brought this boy here?'

The Captain motioned me to a seat, which I took, and sat back himself in his former place.

'Because the boy is going with me, and I thought that you might have something to say to him before he went.'

'Something to say to him?'

The old man repeated the words like a sneer, then he faced on me again and addressed me with an unmoving face.

'Yes, I have something to say to you. Young man, you are going on a fool's errand.'

Captain Marmaduke laughed a little at this, but I could see that he was not pleased.

'Come, brother, don't say that,' he said.

'But I do say it,' the old gentleman repeated. 'A fool's errand it is, and a fool's errand it will be called; and it shall not be said of Nathaniel Amber that he saw his brother make a fool of himself without telling him his mind.'

'I can always trust you for that, Nathaniel,' said the Captain gravely. The old man went on without heeding the interruption.

'A fool's errand I call it, and shall always call it. What a plague! can a man find moneys and a tall ship and stout fellows, and set them to no better use than to found a Fool's Paradise with them at the heel of the world? Ships were made for traffic and shipmen for trade, and not for such whimsies.'

The Captain frowned, but he said nothing, and tapped the toes of his crossed boots with his malacca. But Cornelys Jensen, advancing forward, put in his word.

'Saving your presence, Master Nathaniel,' he said, 'but is not this a most honourable and commendable enterprise? What better thing could a gallant gentleman do than to found such a brotherhood of honest hearts and honest hands as Captain Marmaduke here proposes?'

The frown faded from the Captain's face, and a pleased flush deepened its warm colour. It is a curious thing that men of his kidney—men with an unerring eye for a good man—have often a poor eye for a rogue. It amazed me to see my Captain so pleased at the praisings of Cornelys Jensen. But I was to find out later that he was the easiest man in the world to deceive.

'Spoken like a man, Cornelys; spoken like a true man,' he said.

'I must ever speak my mind,' said Cornelys Jensen. 'I may be a rough sea-fellow, but if I have a thing to say I must needs spit it out, whether it please or pain. And I say roundly here, in your honour's presence, that I think this to be a noble venture, and that I have never, since first I saw salt water, prepared for any cruise with so much pleasure.'

Which was indeed true, but not as he intended my Captain to take it, and as my Captain did take it.

'Well,' grumbled Nathaniel, 'you are a pair of fools, both of you,' and as he spoke he glanced from one to the other with those little shrewd eyes of his, looking at my Captain first and then at Cornelys.

Young as I was, and fresh to the reading of the faces of crafty men, I thought that the look in his eyes—for his face changed not at all—was very different when they rested on the brown face of Cornelys Jensen than when they looked on the florid visage of my good patron. He glanced with contempt upon his kinsman, but I did not see contempt in the gaze he fixed upon Cornelys, who returned his gaze with a steady, unabashed stare.

'Yes,' the old man went on, 'you are a pair of fools, and a fool and his money is a pithy proverb, and true enough of one of you. But it is well sometimes to treat a fool according to his folly, and so, if you are really determined upon this adventure——'

He paused, and looked again at the Captain and again at Cornelys Jensen.

Cornelys Jensen remained perfectly unmoved. The Captain's face grew a shade redder.

'I am,' he said shortly.

'Very well, then,' said the old gentleman; 'as you are my brother, I must needs humour you. You shall have the moneys you need——'

'Now that's talking,' interrupted the Captain.

'Although I know it is a foolhardy thing for me to do.'

'You get good enough security, it seems to me,' said the Captain, a thought gruffly.

'Maybe I do,' said Nathaniel, 'and maybe I do not. Maybe I have a fancy for my fine guineas, and do not care to part with them, however good the security may be.'

'Lord, how you chop and change!' said the Captain. 'Act like a plain man, brother. Will you or will you not?'

'I have said that I will,' said Nathaniel slowly.

I could see that for some reason it amused him to irritate his brother by his reluctance and by his slow speech. The ancient knave knew it for the surest way to spur him to the enterprise.

'When can I have the money?' asked the Captain.

'Not to-day,' said Nathaniel slowly, 'nor yet to-morrow.'

'Why not to-morrow? It would serve me well to-morrow.'

'Very well,' said Nathaniel with a sigh; 'to-morrow it shall be, though you do jostle me vilely.'

'Man alive! I want to be off to sea,' said the Captain.

'The sooner we are off the better,' interpolated Jensen; and once again I noted that Nathaniel shot a swift glance at him through his half-closed lids.

'You are bustling fellows, you that follow the sea life,' said Nathaniel. 'Well, it shall be to-morrow, and I will have all the papers made ready and the money in fat bags, and you will have nothing to do but to sign the one and to pocket the other. And now I must be jogging.'

The Captain made no show of staying him. Nathaniel moved towards the door slowly, weighing up upon his crutched stick.

'Farewell, Marmaduke!' he said. He took the Captain's hand, but soon parted with it.

Then he looked at me.

'Good-day, young fellow,' he said. 'Do not forget that I told you you went on a fool's errand.'

I drew aside to make way for him, and he left the room without a look or a word for Cornelys Jensen. In another minute I saw him through the window hobbling along the street.

He looked malignant enough, but I did not know then how malignant a thing he was. I was ever a weak wretch at figures and business and finance, but it was made plain to me later that Master Nathaniel had so handled Master Marmaduke in this matter of the lending of moneys, that if by any chance anything grave were to happen to Master Marmaduke and to the lad Lancelot and the lass Marjorie all that belonged to Captain Marmaduke would swell the wealth of his brother. And here were Captain Marmaduke and Lancelot and Marjorie all going to sea together and going in company of Cornelys Jensen. And I know now that Master Nathaniel knew Cornelys Jensen very well. But I did not know it then or dream it as I turned from the window and looked at the handsome rascal, who seemed agog to be going.

'Shall you need me longer, Captain?' Jensen asked. 'There is much to do which should be doing.'

'Nay,' said the Captain, 'you are free, for me. I know that there is much to do, and I know that you are the man to do it. But I shall see you in the evening.'

Jensen saluted the Captain, nodded to me, and strode out of the room. Then the Captain sat me down and talked for some twenty minutes of his plan and his hope. If I did not understand much, I felt that I was a fortunate fellow to be in such a glorious enterprise. I wish I had been more mindful of all that he said, but my mind was ever somewhat of a sieve for long speeches, and the dear gentleman spoke at length.

Presently he consulted his watch.

'The coach should be in soon,' he said. 'Let us go forth and await it.'

41

We went out of the Dolphin together into the hall, and there we came to a halt, for he had thought upon some new point in his undertaking, and he began to hold forth to me upon that.

I can see the whole place now—the dark oak walls, the dark oak stairs, and my Captain's blue coat and scarlet face making a brave bit of colour in the sombre place. The Noble Rose is gone long since, but that hall lives in my memory for a thing that just then happened.

CHAPTER X

SHE COMES DOWN THE STAIRS

From the hall of the Noble Rose sprang an oak staircase, and at this instant a girl began to descend the stairs. She was quite young—a tall slip of a thing, who scarcely seemed nineteen—and she had hair of a yellow that looked as if it loved the sun, and her eyes were of a softer blue than my friend's. I knew that at last I looked on Marjorie, Lancelot's Marjorie, the maid whose very picture had seemed farther from me than the farthest star. Her face was fresh, as of one who has enjoyed liberally the open air, and not sat mewed within four walls like a town miss. I noted, too, that her steps as she came down the stairs were not taken mincingly, as school-girls are wont to walk, but with decision, like a boy.

Indeed, though she was a beautiful girl, and soon to make a beautiful woman, there was a quality of manliness in her which pleased me much then and more thereafter. There is a play I have seen acted in which a girl goes to live in a wood in a man's habit. I have thought since that she of the play must have showed like this girl, and indeed I speak but what I know when I say that man's apparel became her bravely. Now, as she came down the stairs she was clad in some kind of flowered gown of blue and white which set off her fair loveliness divinely. She carried some yellow flowers at her girdle; they were Lent lilies, as I believe.

This apparition distracting my attention from the Captain's words, he wheeled round upon his heel and learnt the cause of my inattention. Immediately he smiled and called to the maiden.

'Come here, niece; I have found you a new friend.'

She came forward, smiling to him, and then looked at me with an expression of the sweetest gravity in the world. Surely there never was such a girl in the world since the sun first shone on maidens.

'Lass,' said the Captain, 'this is our new friend. His name is Raphael Crowninshield, but, because I think he has more of the man in him than of the archangel, I mean to call him Ralph.'

The girl held out her hand to me in a way that reminded me much of Lancelot.

As I took her hand I felt that my face was flaming like the sun in a sea-fog— no less round and no less red. I was timid with girls, for I knew but few, and after my misfortune I had shunned those few most carefully. She was not shy

43

herself, though, and she did not seem to note my shyness—or, if she did, it gave her no pleasure to note it, as it would have given many less gracious maidens. Her hand was not very small, but it was finely fashioned—a noble hand, like my Captain's and like Lancelot's; a hand that gave a true grasp; a hand that it was a pleasure to hold.

'Shall I call you Ralph or Raphael?' she said.

My face grew hotter, and I stammered foolishly as I answered her that I begged she would call me by what name she pleased, but that if it pleased my Captain to call me Ralph, then Ralph I was ready to be.

'Well and good, Ralph,' she said.

We had parted hands by this time, but I was still staring at her, full of wonder.

'This boy,' said the Captain, 'goes with us in the Royal Christopher. We will find our New World together. He is a good fellow, and should make a good sailor in time.'

As the Captain spoke of me and the girl looked at me I felt hotter and more foolish, and could think of nothing to say. But even if I could have thought of anything to say I had no time to say it in, for there came an interruption which ended my embarrassment; a horn sounded loudly, and every soul in Sendennis knew that the coach was in.

In a moment everything was changed. The Captain took his hand from my shoulder; the girl took her gaze from my face. There was a clatter of wheels, a trampling of horses' hoofs. The coach had drawn up in front of the inn door. We three—my Captain, the girl, and myself—ran across the hall and out on the portico. There was the usual crowd about the newly arrived coach; but there was only one person in the crowd for whom we looked, and him we soon found.

A lithe figure in a buff travelling coat swung off the box-seat, and Lancelot was with us again. He had an arm around the girl's neck, and kissed her with no heed of the people; he had a hand clasped between the two hands of the Captain, who squeezed his fingers fondly. Then he looked at me, and leaving his kindred he caught both my hands in both his, while his joy shone in his eyes.

'Raphael, my old Raphael, is it you?' he said; 'but my heart is glad of this.'

I wrung his hands. I could scarcely speak for happiness at seeing him again.

'You must not call him Raphael any more,' the girl said demurely. 'He is to be Ralph now, for all of us, so my uncle says.'

'Is that so?' said Lancelot, looking up at the Captain. 'Well, we must obey orders, and indeed I would rather have Ralph than Raphael. 'Tis less of an outlandish name.'

Then we all laughed, and we all came back into the hall of the inn together.

I watched Lancelot with wonder and with pride. He had grown amazingly in the years since I had seen him, and carried himself like a man. He was handsomer than ever I thought, and liker to our island's patron saint. As he stripped off his travelling coat and stood up in the neat habit of a well-to-do town gentleman, he looked such a cavalier as no woman but would wish for a lover, no man but desire for a friend.

'Lads and lass,' said Captain Amber, 'it will soon be time to dine. We have waited dinner for this scapegrace'—and he pinched Lancelot's ear—'so get the dust of travel off as quickly as may be, and we will sit down with good appetite.'

At these words I made to go away, for I did not dream that I was to be of the party; but the Captain, seeing my action, caught me by the arm.

'Nay, Ralph,' he said, 'you must stay and dine with us. You are one of us now, and Lancelot must not lose you on this first day of fair meeting.'

I was indeed glad to accept, for Lancelot's sake. But there was another reason in my heart which made me glad also, and that reason was that I should see the girl again who was my Captain's darling, the sister whom Lancelot had kissed.

So I said that I would come gladly, if so be that I had time to run home and tell my mother, lest she might be keeping dinner for me.

'That's right, lad, that's right. Ever think of the feelings of others.'

My Captain was always full of moral counsels and maxims of good conduct, but they came from him as naturally as his breath, and his own life was so honourable that there was nothing sanctimonious in his way or his words.

As I was about to start he begged me to assure my mother that if she would join them at table he would consider it an honour. I thanked him with tears in my eyes, and saluting them all I left the inn quickly, with the last sweet smile of that girl's burning in my memory.

CHAPTER XI

A FEAST OF THE GODS

I sped through the streets to our house as swiftly, I am sure, as that ancient messenger of the Pagan gods—he that had the wings tied to his feet that he might travel the faster. My dear mother was rejoiced at the Captain's kindness, but she would by no means hear of coming with me. She bade me return with speed, that I might not keep the company waiting, and to thank the Captain for her with all my heart for his kindness and condescension.

When I got back to the Noble Rose I found our little company all assembled in the Dolphin. No one stayed my entrance this time, for though the same fellow that I had tussled with before saw me enter he made no objection this time, and even saluted me in a loutish manner; for I was the Captain's friend, and as such claimed respect.

Lancelot was leaning against the mantelpiece, and Marjorie and my Captain were sitting by plying him with questions and listening eagerly to his answers. Lancelot had drawn off his travelling boots and spruced himself, and looked a comely fellow. When I entered he broke off in what he was saying to clasp my hand again, while the Captain rang for dinner, expressing as he did so the civilest regrets at my mother's absence. Then we all sat to table and dined together in the pleasantest good-fellowship.

Never shall I forget that dinner, not if I live to be a hundred—which is not unlikely, for I come of a long-lived race by my mother's side, and winds and waters have so toughened me that I ought to last with the best of my ancestors. There was a Latin tag Mr. Davies used to tease me with about the Feasts of the Gods. Feasts of the Gods, forsooth! They could not compare, I'll dare wager, with that repast in the Dolphin Room of the Noble Rose, on that crisp spring day when I and the world were younger.

I might well be excused, a raw provincial lad, if I did feel shyish in the presence of such gentlefolk. But they were such true gentlefolk that it was impossible for long not to feel at ease in their society. So when I learnt that Lancelot had not changed one whit in his love for me, and when I found that not the Captain alone, but his beautiful niece too, did everything to make me feel happy and at home—why, it would have been churlish of me not to have aided their gentleness by making myself as agreeable as might be.

"He Broke Off in What He Was Saying To Clasp My Hand."

The Captain had so much to say of his scheme or dream, and we were so content to listen like good children, that we did not rise from table till nigh three o'clock. It was such a happy dream, and so feelingly depicted by the Captain, that it never occurred to me for a moment to doubt in any wise its feasibility, or to feel aught but sure that I was engaged in the greatest undertaking wherein man had ever shared. When we did part at last, on the understanding that I was to attend upon the Captain daily, I shook hands with Marjorie as with an old friend. I was for shaking hands with Lancelot, too, but he would not hear of it. He would walk home with me, he said; he could not lose me so soon after finding me again. So we issued out of the Noble Rose together, arm-in-arm, in very happy mind.

We walked for a few paces in silence, the sweet silence that often falls upon long-parted friends when their hearts are too full for parley. Then Lancelot asked me suddenly 'Is she not wonderful?' and I could answer no more than 'indeed,' for she seemed to me the most wonderful creature the world had ever seen, which opinion I entertain and cherish to this very day and hour.

'Is she not better than her picture in little?' he questioned, and again I had no more to say than 'indeed,' though I would have liked to find other words for my thoughts. By this time we had come to the way where I should turn to my home, but here Lancelot would needs have it that we should go and visit Mr. Davies's shop in the High Street. I must say that this resolve somewhat smote my conscience, for it was many a long day since I had crossed Mr. Davies's threshold; but I would not say Lancelot nay, and so we went our ways to the High Street and Mr. Davies's shop. And indeed I am glad we did so.

CHAPTER XII

MR. DAVIES'S GIFTS

Mr. Davies did not seem at all surprised to see us when we entered, and he turned round and faced us.

The poor little man had lived so long among his musty books that the real world had become as it were a kind of dream to him, wherein people came like shadows and people went like shadows, and where still the battered battalions of his books abided with him.

But he seemed very well pleased to see us, and shook us both warmly by the hands and called us by our right names, without confounding either of us with the other, and had us into his little back parlour and pressed strong waters upon us, all very hospitably.

Of the strong waters Lancelot and I would have none, for in those days I never touched them, nor did Lancelot. I never drank aught headier than ale in the time when I used to frequent the Skull and Spectacles, and as for Lancelot, who was a gentleman born and used to French wines, he had no relish for more ardent liquors. Then he begged we would have a dish of tea, of which he had been given a little present, he said, of late; and as it would have cut him to the heart if we had refused all his proffers, we sat while he bustled about at his brew, and then we all sipped the hot stuff out of porcelain cups and chatted away as if the world had grown younger.

Mr. Davies was full of curiosity about our departure and the Captain's purpose, and did not weary of putting questions to us, or rather to Lancelot, for he soon found that I knew but little of our business beyond the name of the ship. To be sure, I do not think that Lancelot really knew much more about it than I did, but he could talk as I never could talk, and he made it all seem mighty grand and venturesome and heroic to the little bookseller.

When we rose Mr. Davies rose with us and followed us into the shop, when he insisted that each of us should have a book for a keepsake. He groped along his shelves, and after a little while turned to us with a couple of volumes under his arm.

Mr. Davies addressed Lancelot very gravely as he handed him one of the volumes.

'Master Lancelot,' he said, 'in giving you that book I bestow upon you what is worth more than a king's ransom—yea, more than gold of Ophir and peacocks and ivory from Tarshish, and pearls of Tyre and purple of Sidon. It is John Florio's rendering of the Essays of Michael of Montaigne, and there is no better book in the world, of the books that men have made for men, the books that have no breath of the speech of angels in them. Here may a man learn to be brave, equable, temperate, patient, to look life—aye, and the end of life—squarely in the face, to make the most and best of his earthly portion. Take it, Master Lancelot; it is the good book of a good and wise gentleman, and in days long off, when I am no more, you may remember my name because of this my gift and be grateful.'

Then he turned to me and handed me the other book that he had been hugging under his arm.

'For you, my dear young friend,' he said, 'I have chosen a work of another temper. You have no bookish habit, but you have a gallant spirit, and so I will give you a gallant book.'

He opened the volume, which was a quarto, and read from its title-page in his thin, piping voice, that always reminded me somewhat of his own old bullfinch.

'A New, Short, and Easy Method of Fencing; or, the Art of the Broad and Small Sword, Rectified and Compendiz'd, wherein the practice of these two weapons is reduced to so few and general Rules that any Person of indifferent Capacity and ordinary Agility of Body may in a very short time attain to not only a sufficient Knowledge of the Theory of this art, but also to a considerable adroitness in practice, either for the Defence of his life upon a just occasion, or preservation of his Reputation and Honour in any Accidental Scuffle or Trifling Quarrel. By Sir William Hope of Balcomie, Baronet, late Deputy-Governor of the Castle of Edinburgh.'

I should not have carried such a string of words in my memory merely from hearing Mr. Davies say them over once. But they and the book they spoke of became very familiar to me afterwards, and I know it and its title by root of heart.

Lancelot thanked him for us both in well-chosen words, such as I should never have found if I had cudgelled my brains for a fortnight.

Then we wrung Mr. Davies's hands again, and he wished us God-speed, and we came out again into the open street, where the day had now well darkened down.

As we walked along the High Street with our books under our arms Lancelot gave me many particulars concerning his uncle's scheme and his means for furthering it.

It would appear that Captain Marmaduke had for some time cherished the notion of an ideal colony. The thought came originally into his head, so Lancelot fancied, from his study of such books as the 'Republic' of Plato and the 'Utopia' of Sir Thomas More, works I had then never heard of, and have found no occasion since that time to study. But, as I gathered from Lancelot, they were volumes that treated of ideal commonwealths.

Captain Amber's first idea, it appeared, was to establish his little following in one of His Majesty's American colonies. But while he was in the Low Countries he had heard much of those new lands at the end of the world, wherein the Dutch are so much interested, and it seems that the Dutch Government, in gratitude to him for some services rendered, were willing to make him a concession of land wherein to try his venture. At least I think, as well as I can remember, that this was so; I know that somehow or other the Dutch Government was mixed up in the matter.

What further resolved Captain Amber to go so far afield was, it seems, the friendship he had formed while at Leyden with Cornelys Jensen. This Jensen was a fellow of mixed parentage, a Dutch father and an English mother, who had followed the sea all his life, and knew, it seemed, very intimately those parts of the world whereto Captain Amber's thoughts were turned.

Jensen was such a plausible fellow, and professed to be so enraptured with Captain Amber's enterprise, that the Captain's heart was quite won by the fellow, and from that time out he and Cornelys Jensen were hand and glove together in the matter. Very valuable Jensen proved, according to the Captain; full of experience, expeditious, and a rare hand at the picking up of stout fellows for a crew. I found that Lancelot did not hold him in such high regard as his uncle did, but that out of respect for Captain Amber's judgment he held his peace.

As for the Captain's brother Nathaniel, his whole share in the enterprise consisted in the advancing of moneys, on those ungentle terms I have recorded, upon the broad lands and valuables which made my Captain a man of much worldly gear.

Lancelot brought me to my door, we still talking of this and of that.

Lancelot came within for a little while and kissed my mother, who hung on his neck for a moment and then cried a little softly, while Lancelot spoke to her with those words of grave encouragement which seemed beyond his years. Then he wished us good-night, and I saw him to the door, and stood watching his tall form stepping briskly up the street in the clear starlight.

The girl I spoke of but now, she in the play-book who lived like a man in the greenwood, says—or bears witness that another said—that none ever loved who loved not at first sight. This was true in my case. For that unhappy business with the girl Barbara, though it was love sure enough, was not such gracious love as that day entered into me and has ever since dwelt with me.

Of course I had much to tell my mother and she listened, as interested as a child in a fairy tale to all that had been said and done in the Noble Rose. But most of all she seemed surprised to hear that a girl was going to sea with us. She questioned me suddenly when I had made an end of my story:

'What do you think of this maid Marjorie, Raphael?'

I felt at the mention of her name that the blood ran red in my face and I was glad to think that the light in the room was not bright enough to betray me, for I felt shy and angry at my shyness and knew that my cheeks flamed for both reasons. But I tried to say unconcernedly that truly Captain Amber was much blessed in such a niece and Lancelot in such a sister. Yet while I answered I felt both hot and cold, as I have felt since with the ague in the Spanish Islands.

We spoke no more of Marjorie that evening but at night I lay long hours awake thinking of her, and when at last I fell asleep I slipped into dreams of her, with her yellow hair, and the yellow flowers in her girdle and the kindness of Heaven in her steadfast eyes.

There are many kinds of love in the world, as there are many kinds of men and many kinds of women, but my love for Marjorie Amber was of the best kind that a man can feel, and it made a man of me.

I have lived a wild life and a vagrant life, I know; but, anyway, my way of life has been a clean way. I have never been a brawler nor a sot, and I have never struck a man to his hurt unless when peril forced me. I have never fought in wantonness or bad blood, but only out of some necessity that would not be said nay to. And, indeed, there have been times when I have let a man live to my own risk. So I hope when my ghost meets elsewhere with the ghosts of my enemies that they will offer me their shadowy fingers in proof that they bear me no malice and are aware that all was done according to honourable warfare. There is the blood of no vindictive death upon my fingers. What blood there is was blood spilt honestly, in a gentlemanly way, in a soldierly way; and there is a blessed Blood that will cleanse me of its stain.

That I can make this boast I owe in all thankfulness to two women. To my mother first, and then to the girl who came to me at the very turn of my life. If I can say truthfully that year in and year out my life has been a fairly creditable one for a man that has followed fortune by sea and by land the Recording Angel must even set it down to the credit of Marjorie.

CHAPTER XIII

TO THE SEA

From that out the days ran by with a marvellous swiftness. There was much to do daily; in my humble way I had to get my sea-gear ready, which kept my dear mother busy; and every day I was with Captain Marmaduke and Lancelot and Marjorie, and every day we all worked hard to get ready for the great voyage and to bring our odd brotherhood together.

It certainly was a strange fellowship which Captain Amber had gathered together to sail the seas in the Royal Christopher.

Most of them were quiet folk of the farming favour, well set up, earnest, with patient faces. There were men who had been old soldiers; there were men who had served with Captain Amber. These were to be the backbone of his colony. Some brought wives, some sisters; altogether we had our share of women on board, about a dozen in all, including the woman whose care it was to wait upon the Captain's niece.

But I did not see a great deal of them, for they lay aft, and it was my Captain's pleasure that I should dwell in his part of the ship; and he himself, though he carried them to a new world and to warmer stars, did not mingle much with them on shipboard. For my Captain had his notion of rank and place, as a man-at-arms should have. He passed his wont in admitting me to his intimacy, and that was for Lancelot's sake.

As for the hands, the finding of them had been, it would seem, chiefly entrusted to the hands of Cornelys Jensen. I saw nothing of them until the day we sailed. What I saw of them then gave me no great pleasure, for several reasons. Many of them were fine-looking fellows enough. All were stalwart, sea-tested, skilled at their work; most seemed jovial of blood and ready to tackle their work cheerily. Some of them were known to me by sight and even by name, for Cornelys Jensen had culled them from the sea-dogs and sea-devils who drank and diced at the Skull and Spectacles. That was not much; many good seamen were familiars of the Skull and Spectacles. But what I misliked in them was the regard they seemed to pay to the deeds and words of Cornelys Jensen. It was but natural, indeed, that they should pay him regard, seeing that he was the second in command after Captain Amber. But it seemed to me then, or perhaps I imagine—judging by the light of later times —that it seemed to me then that their behaviour showed that they looked upon Jensen rather than my Captain as the centre of authority in the ship. Certainly most of them were more of the kidney of Cornelys Jensen than of Marmaduke Amber.

I ventured to break something of my thought to Captain Amber, but he laughed at me for my pains, saying that Jensen was a proper man and very trustworthy, and a man with a better eye for a good seaman than any other man in the kingdom. So I had no more to say, and Cornelys Jensen went his own way and collected his own following unhindered.

Whatever I might think of the crew, there was but one thought for the ship. A finer than the Royal Christopher at that time I had never seen of her kind and size. She was a large ship of the corvette kind, with something of the carack and something of the polacca about her. We boast greatly of our progress in the art of putting tall ships together, and, if we go on at the rate at which, according to some among us, we are going, Heaven only knows where it will end, or with what kind of marine monsters we shall people the great deep. But I cannot think that we have done or ever shall do much better in shipbuilding than we did in the days when I was young.

The hands of the clock wheeled in their circle, and the day came when all was ready and we were to sail.

I was leaning over the side, looking at the downs and the town where I had lived all my life, and which, perhaps, I might never see again. My mother was by my side, and we were talking together as people talk who love each other when a parting is at hand. All of a sudden I became aware of a boat that was pulling across the water in the direction of our ship. It contained a man and a woman, and when it came alongside I saw who the man and the woman were, and saw that they were known to me; and for a moment my heart stood still, and I make no doubt that my face flushed and paled. For the woman was that girl Barbara who had made the Skull and Spectacles so dear and so dreadful to me, and the man was that red-bearded fellow who had clipped her closely in his arms on the day when I went there for the last time. The man who was rowing the boat was none other than the landlord of the Skull and Spectacles, Barbara's uncle.

I drew back before they had noticed me, and I drew my mother away with me. The pair came on board, but I kept my back turned, and they went aft without noting me. It would seem as if Cornelys Jensen had been but waiting for them to set sail, for now he gave the order that all should leave the ship who were not sailing with her. Then there was such sobbings and embracings and hand-claspings ere the relatives and friends who were staying on shore got down the side into the craft that was waiting for them. My mother and I parted somehow, and I saw her safely into the dinghy which I had chartered for her benefit, handled by a waterside fellow whom I knew well for a steady oar.

Everything then seemed to happen with the quickness of a dream. One moment I seemed to see her sitting in the stern of the boat, waving her handkerchief to me; then next there came a rush of tears, that blotted out everything, my mother and the town and all; the next, as it seemed to me, though of course the interval was longer, we were cutting the water with a fair wind, and the downs and the cliffs seemed to be racing away from us. The Royal Christopher had set sail for its haven at the other end of the world.

CHAPTER XIV

THE SEA LIFE

The fair weather with which we were favoured during the early part of our voyage made the time very delightful and very instructive to me. Indeed, I learnt more during those happy weeks of matters that are proper for a man to know than I had even guessed at in the whole course of my life. For the Captain, who was an accomplished swordsman, and Lancelot, who was a promising pupil, were at great pains to teach me the use both of the small sword and the broadsword, at which they exercised me daily upon the deck. Captain Amber had a great regard for Sir William Hope of Balcomie's book, wherein I made my daily study, and he or Lancelot would make me practise all that I read.

I was ever apt at picking up all things wherein strength and skill counted for more than book-learning, and I am glad to think that they found me an apt pupil. Indeed, before we had got half-way on our journey I was almost as pretty a swordsman as Lancelot, and the Captain used often to declare that in time I should be better than he himself was. But this, of course, he said only to encourage me, for indeed I think I have never seen a better master of his weapon than Captain Amber, and neither I nor Lancelot ever came near him in that art.

Captain Amber was my teacher in other things than swordcraft. He set himself with a patience that knew no limit to make me learn such things as are useful in the sea life, and indeed he found me an apter pupil than poor Mr. Davies had ever been able to make of me. He was himself versed in the mathematical sciences, in navigation, in astronomy, dialling, gauging, gunnery, fortification, the use of the globes, the projection of the sphere upon any circle, and many another matter essential for the complete sailor, soldier, or navigator and adventurer of any kind.

He instructed me further in matters military, for, as he said, a stout man should be able to serve God and his King as well by land as by sea. So he put me through a rare course of martial education, discoursing to me very learnedly on the principles of fortification as they are expounded by the ingenious Monsieur Vauban, and showing me, in the plans of many and great towns, both French and German, to what perfection their defence may be carried. He showed me how to handle a musket and a pike, and the manage of the half-pike joined to the musket, and instructed me in the drilling of troops and in the forming of a brigade after the Swedish method, for which he had a particular affection.

He harangued me much upon the uses of artillery, illustrating what he said by the example of the ship's cannon, until I felt that I should only need a little practice to become a master gunner. And he set forth to me by precept—for here he had no chance of example—drill of cavalry and the importance of that arm in war, and promised me that I should learn to ride when we had reached our Arcadia.

In all these exercises Lancelot, whose cabin I shared, took his part. He knew so much more than I did that I feel very sure that my companionship in these studies was but a drag upon him. Yet he never betrayed the least impatience with me or with my more sluggish method of acquiring knowledge. Now, as always, he was my true friend. If every day taught me more to admire Captain Marmaduke, every day bade me the more and more to congratulate myself upon being blessed with such a comrade as Lancelot.

Nevertheless, the best part of the business was the presence of Marjorie. She was a true child of the sea. She loved it as if she had been such a mermaiden as old poets fable. She had sailed with her uncle ever since she was a little girl. She was as good a sailor as her brother, and took foul weather as gallantly as fair. For it was not all smooth sailing, for all our luck. There were squalls and there were storms; but the Royal Christopher rode the billows bravely, and Marjorie faced the storm as fearlessly as the oldest hand on board.

There was one wild night, when we rose and fell in a fury of wind. She must needs be on deck, so I fastened her to one of the masts with a rope and held on next to her while we watched the war of the elements. The rain was strong, and it soaked all the clothes on her body to a pulp; and her long hair floated on the wind, and sometimes flapped across my face and made my blood tingle. She stuck to her post like a man—or, let me say in her honour, like a woman—watching the strife, and every now and then she would put her lips close to my ear—for the screaming of the wind whistled away all words that were not so spoken—and would bid me note some wonder of sky or water. For by this time we were great friends, Marjorie and I, and she always treated me as if I were some kinsman of her house instead of what I was, a poor adventurer in the dawn of his first adventure. She liked me I knew from the start because Lancelot liked me, and because she trusted in Lancelot with the same implicit faith that he addressed to her. And where she liked she liked wholly, as a generous man might, giving her friendship freely in the firm clasp of her hand, in the keen, even greeting of her eyes. It was a strange grace for me to share in that wonderful fellowship of brother and sister, and I joyed in my fortune and shut my mind against any thought of the sorrow that might come to me from such sweet intercourse. For I knew from the first as I have said that I loved her, and I knew, too, that it would be about as reasonable to fall in love with a star or a dream. Those gentry who write verses, find, as I believe, a kind of bitter satisfaction in recording their pains in rhyme, but for me there was no such solace. Yet on that driving night, in that high wind, I would have rejoiced to be apprenticed to the poets' guild and skilled to make some use that might please her of the dumb thoughts that troubled me. As it was it was she who seemed to speak with the speech of angels and I who listened mumchance.

She had the rarest gifts and graces for gladdening our voyage. She could sing, and she could play a guitarra that she had brought from Spain; and often of fair evenings, when we sat out on the deck, she would sing to us ballads in Spanish and French, and then for me, who was unlettered, she would sing old English ditties, such as 'Barbara Allen' and 'When first I saw your face,' and many canzonets from out of Mr. William Shakespeare's plays, which she always held in high esteem, and I would sit and listen in a rapture.

Once, a long while after, when that Spanish tongue had become as familiar to me as it was then unfamiliar, I remember falling into a brawl with a stout fellow in Spain, and getting, as luck would have it, the better of the business, and being within half a mind of ramming my knife into his throat; for my blood was up, and the fellow had meant to kill me if he had had the chance. But even as I made to strike, he, looking up at me, and as cool as if I were doing him a favour, began to sing very softly to himself just one of those very Spanish songs that Marjorie used to sing of summer evenings on the deck of the Royal Christopher. And as he sang so, waiting death, in that instant all my rage vanished, and I put aside my weapon and held out my hand to him, and asked his forgiveness and asked his friendship. The man looked amazed, as well he might; and it was lucky for me that he did not seize the chance to stab me unawares. But he did not, and we shook hands and parted, and he went his ways never witting that he owed his life to the fairest woman in the whole wide world—at least, that I have ever seen, and I have seen many and many in my time.

There were two on that ship with whom I did not wish to have any dealings, namely, Barbara and the red-bearded man, Hatchett by name, who was now her husband. However, I saw but little of them, for they kept to their own part of the ship.

Barbara knew me again, of course, and we saluted each other when we met, as it was of course inevitable that we should meet on board ship. But we did not meet often, and I was glad to find that I felt no pang when the rare meetings did take place. That folly had wholly gone. There—I have written those words, but I have no sooner written than I repent them. It is not a folly for a boy to be honestly in love, as I was in love with Barbara. I was silly, if you please—a moon-struck, calf-loving idiot, if you like—but in all that hot noon of my madness there never was an unclean thought in my mind nor an unclean prompting of the body. However, all that was past and done with. My liver was washed clean of that passion; it had not left a spot upon my heart. I have only loved two women in all my life, and when the second love came into my life that first fancy was dead and buried, and no other fancy has ever for a moment arisen to trouble my happiness.

CHAPTER XV

UTOPIA HO!

I have purposely left out of these pages the record of the voyage. One such voyage is much like another, and though it was all new to me it would not be new to others. I might like to dwell again upon the first land we made, the Island of St. Jago, where we had civil entertainment of a Portuguese gentleman and of a negro Romish priest, with a merry heart and merry heels. My mother would have loved to go marketing in that place, for I bought no less than one hundred sweet oranges for half a paper of pins, and five fat hens for the other half of the paper. I could talk of our becalms and our storms and our crossing the Line, and of our trouble with the travado-wind. But as I do not wish to weary with the repetition of an oft-told tale, I will say no more of our voyage until we came to the Cape which is so happily named of Good Hope. It was a very wonderful voyage for me; it would not seem a very wonderful voyage to others, who have either made it themselves or who know out of book knowledge all and more than all that I could tell them. But I may say that I was a very different lad when we came to the Cape from the lad who had got on board of the Royal Christopher so many months earlier. I was but a pale-faced boy when I sailed, only a landsman, and no great figure as a landsman. But when we came to the Cape I was so coloured by the winds and the suns and the open life that my face and hands were well-nigh of the tint of burnished copper. I had always been a fairly strong lad; but now my strength was multiplied many times, and, thanks to my dear master, my skill to use that strength was marvellously advanced. Which proved to be of infinite service to me and others better than myself by-and-by.

We stayed some little time at Cape Town; how long now I do not closely remember, but, as I think, a matter of four weeks or more. For the Captain had some old friends amongst the Dutch colony, and there were certain matters of revictualling the ship to be thought of, and Lancelot longed for a little shooting and hunting. For my part, I was by no means loth to tread the soil again, for, though I love the sea dearly, I have no hatred for firm earth as other seamen have, but look upon myself as a kind of amphibious animal, and like the land and the water impartially. And there was a great joy and wonder to me to see a new country and a new town—I, who knew of no other town than Sendennis, and knew no more of London than of Grand Cairo, or of the capital of the Mogul. I remember that we stayed some days under the roof of a leading Dutch merchant of the place, who entertained us very handsomely, and that his brother, who was a somewhat younger man than he, and who spoke our English tongue well, took Lancelot and me many times a-shooting and a-fishing, and that we had some rare and savage sport. For the town is but a small one, and there is excellent sport to be had well-nigh at its back doors, as it were. I should have loved dearly to have wandered inward far inland towards the great mountains, for I heard wonderful tales, both from the Dutchmen and their black men, of treasures that the bowels of these mountains were said to hold. Of course that was out of the question, with the Royal Christopher waiting for her fate; but the tales fired me with memories of those Eastern tales that I have told you of, and I longed to out-rival Master Sindbad.

I cannot conscientiously affirm that I was sorry to leave Cape Town, and the wines that the Dutch settlers made, and the amazing Hottentots, and the other marvels of that my first experience of strange distant countries. We were all the better for our rest, Marjorie and Captain Amber, Lancelot, the colonists, the crew, and, in a word, all our fellowship. But we were all eager to be on the way again, for very different reasons. Captain Amber, because he was keen to place his foot upon his Land of Promise; Lancelot, because he wished what his uncle wished; Marjorie, because she wished to be with Lancelot; I myself, much out of eager, restless curiosity for new places and new adventures. For I was so simple in those days that the mere crossing of the seas seemed to me to be an adventure, a thing that I came later to regard as no more adventurous than the hiring of a hackney-coach. But in my heart I knew that the main reason for my bliss in boarding the Royal Christopher lay in the closer intimacy it gave me with maid Marjorie. In the little kingdom of the ship, where all in a sense were friends and adventurers together, there was less than on land to remind me that for me to dream myself her lover went far to prove me lunatic. So I was blithe to be afloat again. As for Cornelys Jensen, we were to learn soon enough in what direction lay his pleasure to be ploughing the high seas again.

CHAPTER XVI

I MAKE A DISCOVERY

I have been brief with our adventure so far, because it only began to be adventurous after we had left the Cape leagues behind us. Up to that time, though the voyage was full of wonders for me, it was but one voyage with another for those who use the sea. But when the adventure did begin it began briskly, and having once made a beginning it did not make an end for long enough, nor without great changes of fortune. Yet it began, as a big business often does begin, in a very little matter. One night, somewhat late, Captain Amber wished for a word with Jensen. Yet, as it was not the Dutchman's watch, and he might be sleeping, Captain Amber bade me go to his cabin— for Jensen, being a man of consideration upon the ship, had a cabin to himself —to see if he were stirring, commanding me, however, if he were resting, not to arouse him. Jensen's cabin lay amidships, and as I proceeded warily because of the Captain's caution, I came to it quietly and listened at the door before lifting my finger to knock. As I did so I noticed that the door was not fastened. Whoever had drawn it to had not latched it, and it lay open just a chink, through which a line of light showed from within. Thinking that if I peeped through this chink I might learn if Jensen were astir or no, I put my eye to it and saw what I saw.

The cabin was not a very large one, and though the lamp that swung from the ceiling gave forth but a dim light, yet it was enough to enable me to see very clearly all that there was to see. At the first blush, indeed, there seemed to be nothing out of the way to witness. At the further end of the cabin two men were sitting at a table together, with a chart before them. Nearer to me, and in front of the men, a woman stood, and held up for their inspection a piece of needlework. The two men were Cornelys Jensen and William Hatchett; the woman was Barbara Hatchett. It might have made a very pleasing example of domestic peace but for one queer fact, which notably altered its character.

The needlework at which women are wont to labour is nine times out of ten white work or brightly-coloured work. Women are like the best kind of birds, and love snowy plumage or feathers that are bravely tinted. But the work with which Barbara Hatchett was occupied was neither white nor coloured, but black—the deepest, darkest black. Now there was no cause as yet, thank Heaven! for man or woman to mourn on board of the Royal Christopher, and there was no need for Mistress Barbara to deal with mourning. So I marvelled, but even as I marvelled I noted, as she shifted her position slightly and shook out the black stuff over her knees, that it was not all and only black. There was white work in it too, a kind of patch or pattern of white work in the midst which I could not make out, for the stuff was still bunched up in the woman's hands. But now, as I watched, I saw her shake it out over her knees for the others to view, and I saw that the thing she displayed was a large square of black worsted, and that in the centre were sewn some pieces of white material into a very curious semblance. For that semblance was none other than the likeness of a grinning human skull, with two cross-bones beneath it—just such an effigy as I had seen many times on the tombstones in the churchyard at Sendennis.

"Held Up for Their Inspection a Piece of Needlework."

It was not, however, of the tombstones at Sendennis that I thought just then. No; that ugly image in the girl's fingers carried my fancy back to the place where I had first seen her—to the hostelry of the Skull and Spectacles—and I fancied somehow, I scarce knew why, that the work of Barbara's fingers had some connection with her father's inn. Only for a second or so did I think this, but in honest truth that was my first, my immediate belief, and it brought me no thought of fear, no thought of danger with it. I was only conscious of wondering vaguely to what service this sad piece of handicraft could be put, when suddenly, in a flash, my intelligence took fire, and I knew what was intended; and I felt my knees give way and my heart stand still with horror.

The thing I was looking at, the ill-favoured thing that was hanging from my old love's hand, was none other than a flag of evil omen—a pirate's flag, the barbarous piece of bunting that they call the Jolly Roger. There could be no doubt of that—no doubt whatever. I had heard of that flag and read of it, and now I was looking at it with my own eyes; and a light seemed to be let in upon my mind, and I trembled at the terror it brought with it. That piece of handicraft meant murder; meant outrage; meant violence of all kinds to those that were so dear to me—to those who were all unconscious of their imminent doom. For I was as sure now as if those three had told it to me with their own lips that I had come upon a conspiracy.

The red-haired ruffian and the black-haired ruffian were in a tale together; their purpose was to seize the poor Royal Christopher that sailed on so gentle an errand and make her a pirate ship, with that devil's ensign flying at her forepeak. My soul sickened in my body at the thought of the women-kind at the mercy of these desperadoes. There was one name ever in my heart, and as I thought of that name I shivered as if the summer night had suddenly been frozen. I believe that if I had had a brace of pistols with me I should have taken my chance of sending those two villains out of the world with a bullet apiece, so clearly did their malignity betray itself to my observation. But I was unarmed, and even if I had been I might have missed my aim—though this I do not think likely, in that narrow place, and with my determination steadying my hand—and, moreover, I had no notion as to how many of the ship's crew were sworn to share in the villainy. Besides, I have never killed a man in cold blood in my life, and on that night so long ago I had never lifted hand and weapon against any man, and had only once in my life seen blood spilt murderously. But I stayed there, with my heart drumming against my ribs and my breath coming in gasps that seemed to me to shake the ship's bulk, staring hard at the two men and the woman with her work.

She held out the banner at arm's length, and looked down at it lovingly, as women are wont to look at any piece of needlework that they have taken pains over with pleasure in the pains. I had seen women smile over their work many and many a time—good women that have worked for their kin, mothers that have laboured to fashion some bit of bodygear for a cherished child—and I have always thought that the smile upon their faces was very sweet to see. But in this case there was the same smile upon the woman's face as she looked upon her unholy handiwork, and there was something terrible in the contrast between that look of housewifely satisfaction and the job upon which it was bestowed. Many an evil sight have I seen, but never, as I think, anything so evil as this sight of that beautiful face smiling over the edge of that hideous thing, the living radiant visage above that effigy of death. The black flag covered her like a pall, ominously.

'Well,' she said, 'is it well done?'

She spoke in a low tone, but I could hear what she said quite well where I crouched.

Cornelys Jensen nodded his head approvingly.

The red-bearded man spoke. 'Time it was done, too, and that we should be setting to work. I am sick of this waiting.'

'Patience, my good fellow, patience,' said Cornelys Jensen. 'All in good time. Trust Cornelys Jensen to know the time to act. The fiddle is tuned, friend. I shall know when to play the jig.'

'My feet ache for the dancing,' the red beard growled. Barbara laughed; dropping her hands, she drew the black flag close to her, so that it fell all in folds about her body and draped her from throat to toe. Her beauty laughed triumphantly at the pair from its sable setting.

'Put that thing away,' said Jensen. 'You have done your work bravely, Mistress Hatchett, and Bill may be well proud of you.'

He clapped his hand as he spoke on Red Beard's shoulder, and the fool's face flushed with pleasure.

Barbara laughed, and slowly folded the flag up square by square into a small compass. Jensen took it from her when she had finished and put it into a locker, which he closed with a key that he took from his pocket.

I began to find my position rather perilous. It was high time for me to take my departure, before the conspirators became aware of my whereabouts. It would not trouble either of the men a jot to ram a knife into my ribs and to jerk me overboard ere the life was out of me. And then what would become of my dear ones, and of all the honest folk on board, with no one to warn them of their peril?

I drew back very cautiously, creeping along the passage and holding my breath, stepping as gingerly as a cat on eggs, for fear of making any sound that should betray me. As I crept along I kept asking myself what I was to do. The first course that came to my mind was to go to Captain Marmaduke and tell him of what I had seen. But then, again, I did not know, and he did not know, how many there were of crew or company tarred with Jensen's brush, and I asked myself whether it would not first be more prudent to consult with Lancelot. For I knew that with Captain Marmaduke the first thing he would do would be to accuse Jensen to his face, without taking any steps to countermine him, and then we should have the hornets' nest about our ears with a vengeance.

But while I was creeping along in the dark, straining my ears for every sound that might suggest that Jensen or Hatchett were following me, and while my poor mind was anxiously debating as to the course I ought to pursue, that came to pass which settled the question in the most unexpected manner.

CHAPTER XVII

A VISITATION

My agitations were harshly interrupted. There came a crash out of the silence, and before I could even ask myself what it meant I was flung forward and my legs were taken from under me. I pitched on to a coil of rope, luckily for me, or I might have come to worse hurt, and I had my hands extended, which in a measure broke the force of my fall. But I rapped my head smartly against the wall of the passage—never had I more reason in my life to be grateful for the thickness of my skull—and for a few moments I lay there in the darkness, dizzy—indeed, almost stunned—and scarcely realising that there was the most horrible grinding noise going on beneath me, and that the ship seemed to be screaming in every timber. I could have only lain there for a few seconds, for no human clamour had mingled with the sound of the ship's agony when I staggered to my feet. My head was aching furiously, and my right wrist was numb from the fall, but my senses had now come back to me, and I knew that some great calamity had befallen the ship. In desperation I pulled myself together and ran with all speed, heedless of the darkness, to the end of the passage where the ladder was, and so up it and on to the deck.

The weather was fair, and a moon like a wheel made everything as visible as if it were daytime. The decks shone silver and the sky was as blue as I have ever seen it; but the sea, as far as eye could reach, appeared to be wholly covered with a white froth, which rose and fell with the waves like a counterpane of lace upon a sleeper. All that there was to see I saw in a single glance; in another second the deck was full of people.

Captain Marmaduke came on deck clad only in his shirt and breeches, and Lancelot was by his side a moment after in like habit. At first the sailors rushed hither and thither in alarm and confusion, but Cornelys Jensen brought them to order in a few moments, while Hatchett and half a dozen of the men proceeded to reassure the passengers and to keep them from crowding on to the deck. All this happened in shorter time than I can take to set it down, and yet after a fashion, too, it seemed endless.

Captain Marmaduke rushed up to the watch and caught him by the shoulder. 'What have you done?' he said; 'you have lost the ship!'

The man shook himself away from the Captain's hand.

'It was no fault of mine,' he said between his teeth. 'I took all the care I could. I saw all this froth at a distance, and I asked the steersman what it was, and he told me that it was but the sea showing white under the light of the moon.'

Captain Marmaduke gave a little groan of despair.

'What is to be done?' he asked. 'Where are we?'

'God only knows where we are,' the man answered, still in that sullen, shamefaced way. 'But for sure we are fast upon a bank that I never heard tell of ere this night.'

As they were thus talking, and all around were full of consternation, I saw that Marjorie had come up from below and was standing very still by the companion head. She had flung a great cloak on over her night-rail, and though her face was pale in the moonlight she was as calm as if she were in church. When I came nigh her she asked me, in a low, firm voice, what had happened.

I told her all that I knew—how the ship had by mischance run on some bank through the whiteness of the moonlight misleading the steersman. With another woman, maybe, I should have striven to make as light as possible of the matter, but with Marjorie I knew that there was no such need. I told her all that had chanced and of the peril we were in, as I should have done to a man.

"She Had Flung a Great Cloak on."

When I had done speaking she said very quietly: 'Is there any hope for the ship?'

I shook my head. 'I am very much afraid——' I began.

She interrupted me with a little sigh, and stepped forward to where Captain Marmaduke stood giving his orders very composedly. Lancelot was busy with Jensen in reassuring the women-folk and getting the men-folk into order. I must say that they all behaved very well. With many of the men, old soldiers and sailors as they were, it was natural enough to carry themselves with coolness in time of peril, but the women showed no less bravely. This, indeed, was largely due to the example set them by Barbara Hatchett, who acted all through that wild hour as a sailor's daughter and a sailor's wife should act. Her composure and her loud, commanding voice and encouraging manner did wonders in soothing the women-kind, and in putting out of their heads the foolish thoughts which lead to foolish actions.

Marjorie went up to Lancelot and laid her hand upon his sleeve. He looked at her with the smile he always gave when he greeted her, and he spoke to her as he might have spoken if he and she had been standing together on the downs of Sendennis instead of on that nameless reef in that nameless danger.

'Well, dear,' he said, 'what is it?'

'What do you wish me to do?' she asked.

'Comfort the women-folk, dear,' he answered. Then, catching sight as the wind moved her cloak of her night-rail, he added quickly: 'Run down and dress first.'

'Is there truly time?'

'Aye, aye, time and to spare. We may float the ship yet, God willing. Do as I bid you.'

She lingered for a moment, and said softly:

'If anything should happen, let me be next you at the last.'

I was standing near enough to hear, and the tears came into my eyes. Lancelot caught his sister's hand and pressed it as he would have pressed the hand of a comrade. Then she turned away and slipped silently below.

I am glad to remember that good order prevailed in the face of our common peril. Our colonists, men and women, kept very quiet, and the sailors, under Cornelys Jensen, acted with untiring zeal. I must say to his credit that Jensen proved a cool hand in the midst of a misfortune which must have come as a special misfortune to himself. It is a curious fact, and I know not how to account for it, unless by the smart knock on my head and the confusion of events that followed upon it, but all memory of what I had seen and heard In Jensen's cabin had slipped from my mind. No—I will not say all memory. While I watched him working, and while I worked with him, my head— which still ached sorely after my tumble—was troubled, besides its own pain, with the pain of groping after a recollection. I knew that there was something in my mind which concerned Cornelys Jensen, something which I wanted to recall, something which I ought to recall, something which I could not for the life of me recall. What with my fall, and the danger to the ship, and the strain of the toil to meet that danger, that page of my memory was folded over, and I could not turn it back. I have heard of like cases and even stranger; of men forgetting their own names and very identity after some such accident as mine. All I had forgotten was the evil scene in Jensen's cabin, the three evil schemers, their evil flag.

I was a pretty skilled seaman now, thanks to my Captain's patience and my own eagerness, and I was able to lend a hand at the work with the best. The first thing we did was to throw the lead, and sorry information it yielded us.

For we found that we had forty-eight feet of water before the vessel and much less behind her. It was then proposed that we should throw our cannon overboard, in the hope that when our ship was lightened of so much heavy metal she might by good hap be brought to float again. I remember as well as yesterday the face of Cornelys Jensen when this determination was arrived at. He saw that it must be done, but the necessity pricked him bitterly. 'There's no help for it,' he said aloud to Hatchett, with a sigh. Captain Marmaduke took the expression, as I afterwards learnt, as one of pity for him and his ship and her gear of war. But it set me racking my tired brain again for that lost knowledge about Jensen which would have made his meaning plain to me.

It was further decided to let fall an anchor, but while the men were employed upon this piece of work the conditions under which we toiled changed greatly for the worse. Black clouds came creeping up all round the sky, which blotted out the moonlight and changed all that white foam into curdling ink, and with the coming of these clouds the wind began to rise, at first little and moaningly, like a child in pain, and then suddenly very loudly indeed, until it grew to a great storm, that brought with it sheets of the most merciless rain that I had then ever witnessed. Now, indeed, we were in dismal case, wrapped up as we were in all the horrors of darkness, of rain and of wind, which added not merely a gloom to our situation, but vastly increased danger. For our ship, surrounded as she was with rocks and shoals, though she might have lain quiet enough while the sea was calm, now before the fury of the waves kept continually striking, and I could see that the fear of every man was that she would shortly go to pieces.

CHAPTER XVIII

THE NIGHT AND MORNING

It seemed such a heart-breaking thing to be hitched in that place, so immovable, while the seas were slapping us and the wind so foully misbehaving, that I declare I could have wept for bitterness of spirit. But it was no time for weeping; we had other guesswork on hand, and we buckled to our work with a will. We agreed that the straightest course open to us was to cut away the mainmast, and this we promptly set about doing. There are few sadder sights in the world than to see stout fellows striving with all their strength to hew down the mainmast of a goodly ship. The fall of a great tree in a forest preaches its sermon, but not with half the poignancy of a noble mast which men who love their vessel are compelled to cast overboard. As the axes rose and fell it seemed to me as if their every stroke dealt me a hurt at the heart. As the white wood flew it would not have surprised me if blood had followed upon the blow—as I have read the like concerning a tree in some old tale—so dear was the ship to me. A man's first ship is like a man's first love, and grips him hard, and he parts from neither without agony. When at last our purpose was accomplished, and the mast swayed to its fall, I could have sat me down and blubbered like a baby.

And yet in another moment, so strange is the ordering of human affairs and so much irony is there in the lessons of life, we who were all ready to weep for the loss of our mainmast would have been only too glad to say good-bye to it. For while its fall augmented the shock, and made us in worse case that way, we were not lightened of it for all our pains, for it was so entangled with the rigging that we could not for all our efforts get it overboard. We were now in sheer desperation, for it did not seem as if we could ever get our ship free, but must needs bide there in our agony until she broke and gave us all to the waters. But a little after there came a gleam of hope, for the furious wind and rain abated, and finally fell away altogether, and at last the longest night I had ever known came to an end, and the dawn came creeping up to the sky as I had often seen it come creeping when I awakened early lying on my bed in Sendennis. Oh, the joy to hail the daylight again, and yet what a terrible condition of things the daylight showed to us! There was our ship stuck fast on the bank; there was her deck all encumbered with the fallen mast and the twisted ropes and the riven sails. Every man's face was as white as a dish, and there was fear in every man's eyes. Nor was it longer possible to pacify all the women-folk or the children, now that the daylight showed them the full extent of their disaster, and every now and then they would break forth into cries or fits of sobbing which were pitiful to hear. Marjorie did much to calm their terrors, as did Barbara Hatchett, both of whom showed very brave and calm; and, indeed, the only pleasing memory of all that time of terror is the thought of those two women, the one in all the pride of her dark beauty, the other in all the glory of her fair loveliness, moving about like ministering angels amongst all those people whom the sudden peril of death had made so fearful and so helpless. The beautiful woman and the beautiful maid—none on board had braver hearts than they!

You may imagine with what eagerness we scanned the sea for any sight of land. But though Captain Amber searched the whole horizon with his spy-glass, we could find nothing better than an island which lay off from us at a distance of about two leagues, and what seemed to be a smaller island, which lay further from us. This did not offer any great promise of refuge to us, but as it was apparently the only hope we had we all strove to make the best of it, and to pretend to be greatly rejoiced at the sight of even so much land.

Captain Amber immediately ordered Hatchett to man one of the ship's boats and to make for those islands to examine them, a task that now presented no difficulty, for the wind had fallen away and the sea was smooth as it had been turbulent. I would fain have gone with the boat for the sake of the change, for I was sick at heart of the moaning and the groaning of the poor wretches on board, but Captain Amber did not send me, and I had no right to volunteer; and, besides, I was still troubled by a confused sense of something that I had to tell him; some danger that I was instinctively seeking to ward off from him —and from her.

There was something piteous in the sight of that single boat creeping slowly across the sea towards those distant islands, and I watched it as it grew smaller and smaller, until it was little more than a mere speck upon the waters.

Everything depended for us upon the fortunes of that boat, upon the tidings that it might bring back to us. I am proud to say that my thoughts went out across that sea to the home where my mother was, who prayed day and night for her boy's safety, and that my lips repeated that prayer she had taught me while I supplicated Heaven with all humility of heart, if it were His will, to bring us out of that peril.

We spent the time during the boat's absence in clearing the decks as well as we might, in renewing our efforts to pacify our women-kind, and in fresh attempts, which, however, were unavailing, to get our mast overboard. Captain Amber had gathered together those of his men who were old soldiers, and, having addressed them in a stirring speech, which made my blood beat

73

more warmly, he set them to various tasks in preparation for what now appeared to be inevitable—our leaving the ship. The brave fellows behaved as obediently as if they had been on parade, as courageously as if they had been going into action. They were picked men of fine mettle, and they were yet to be tested by severer tests, and to stand the test well.

At about nine o'clock or a little later the boat returned. We could see it, of course, a long way off, as it made its course towards us, but none of those on board made any sign to us, which we took, and rightly, too, to be a sign of no great cheer. Then our hopes, which had begun to run a little higher, ebbed away again, and we waited in silence for the boat to come alongside and for Hatchett to climb on board and to make his report to Captain Marmaduke. This he did in private, Captain Marmaduke taking him a little apart, while we all looked on and hungered for the news.

We had not long to wait, and when it came it was not so bad as we had feared, if it was not so good as some of us had hoped for.

Captain Amber came forward to the middle of the deck, where everybody was assembled waiting for the tidings.

'Friends and companions,' he said, 'our explorers report that yonder island is far from inhospitable. It is not covered by the sea at high water, as we feared at first; it is much larger than it seems to us at this distance; there will be ample room for us all during the short time that we may have to abide there before we sight a ship. I must indeed admit to you that the coast is both rocky and full of shoals, and that the landing thereupon will not be without its difficulties, and even its dangers, but we came out prepared to face difficulties and dangers if needs were, and these shall not dismay us. As for the further island, we may learn of that later.'

He looked very gallant as he said all this, standing there with the morning sunlight shining upon his brave face and upon his fine coat—for by this time he was fully habited and in his best, as beseemeth the leader of an expedition when about to disembark upon an unfamiliar shore. All around him had listened in silence while he spoke, but now, at the close, some of the soldier-fellows set up a kind of cheer in answer to his speech. It was not very much of a cheer, but it was better than nothing in our dismal case. It served to set our bloods tingling a little, so Lancelot and I caught it up, and kept it up too, with the whole strength of our lungs, till the example spread, and soon we had every man on deck huzzaing his best, while Cornelys Jensen and Hatchett swung their caps and lifted their voices with the best. It was a strange sound, that hearty British cheer ringing out through that lonely air; it was a strange sight, all those stout fellows marshalled as best they might on the sloping deck and fanning their scanty hopes into a flame with shouting, while the ruined mast, thrust over the side, pointed curiously enough straight in the direction of those islands whose hospitable qualities we were soon to try.

It was soon decided, after a brief conference between Captain Amber and Cornelys Jensen, that we should transfer our company as fast as might be to the near island, for there was no knowing when the smooth weather might shift again and how long our Royal Christopher would hold together if the waves, which were now lapping against its sides, grew angrier. It was resolved that the most pressing business was to send on shore at once the women and children and such sick people as we had on board, for these, as was but natural, were the most troublesome for us to deal with in our difficulty, being timorous and noisy with their fears, and setting a bad example.

So when it was about ten of the clock, or maybe later, for the time slipped by rapidly, we got loose our shallop and our skiff and lowered them into the water, and got most of the women and the children and the sick folk into them and sent them off, poor creatures, across the waste of waters to the islands. Barbara Hatchett went with them, for her firmness and courage served rarely to keep them quiet and inspire them with some little fortitude. As for Marjorie, she would by no means leave the ship so long as Lancelot was on board, so she stayed with us, at which I could not help in my heart being glad, in spite of the danger that there was to everyone who stuck by the ship.

While these first boat loads were away we on board made efforts for the provisioning of our new home, getting up the bread and such viands as we could, and packing them in as portable a manner as might be for the next journey. But by this time unhappily we began to be threatened by a fresh trouble. No sooner were we free from the women-folk and the children, whose presence had hampered us so sorely, than a far more pressing vexation came upon us. For certain of the sailors, who up to this point had behaved well enough, suddenly flung aside their good behaviour. They had got at the wine, of which, unhappily, in the first confusion of our mischance no care had been taken, and many of them were roaring drunk, and capable of doing little service beyond shouting and cursing at one another. When Cornelys Jensen saw this he did his best to prevent them, and though some of them were too sullen to obey him, he did at last contrive with threats and oaths to keep such of the sailors as were still sober away from the liquor. By this time Lancelot, facing the new danger, got from his uncle the key of the storeroom where the arms were kept, and served out weapons to all those on board who had been soldiers and who loved Captain Amber. A pretty body of men they made, each with a musket on his shoulder, a hanger by his side, and a brace of pistols in his belt. They were all reliable men—many of them, indeed, had experienced religion, and had in them something of the old Covenanting spirit, which had worked such wonders under General Cromwell.

I could see that Cornelys Jensen was very ill-pleased with this act on our part, but he could say nothing, for the thing was done before he could say or do aught to prevent it, and very fortunate it was that we had done so betimes, for now Captain Marmaduke had under him a body of sober, disciplined, well-armed men, who would obey him and stand by him to the last extremity. I myself had slung a hanger by my side and thrust a brace of pistols into my girdle, and I believe that I well-nigh rejoiced in the peril which gave me the chance to carry those weapons and to make, as I fancied, so brave a show. Lancelot armed himself too in like fashion, for he served as second in command of our little troop under Captain Amber. For my part, I held no rank indeed in the little army, but I looked upon myself as a kind of *aide-de-camp* to my Captain.

With half a dozen of those men we gathered together all the cases of wine that had been brought out and placed them back in the spirit room, over which we mounted two men as guard. It was idle to try and lock the door, for the lock had been shattered, possibly when we ran aground, and would not hold. But we locked the door of the room where our weapons and ammunition were, and placed another guard there.

I think many of the sailors were mightily annoyed at this action of ours, and gladly would have resented it. But there was nothing they could do just then, and though Cornelys Jensen was more savage than any of them, he wore a smooth face, and kept them in check by his authority. Though we did not dream of it then, it was a mighty blessing for us, that same shipwreck, for if it had not come about just when it did worse would have happened. As matters now stood, our little party—for it was becoming pretty plain that there were two parties in the ship—was well-armed, while the sailors had no other weapons than their knives.

CHAPTER XIX

HOW SOME OF US GOT TO THE ISLAND

But between our need for watchfulness and the drunkenness of many of the crew the time slipped away without our doing as much as we should have done under happier conditions. Thanks to the confusion that their wantonness had caused, we did but make three trips in all to the island in that day, in which three trips we managed to send over about fifty persons, with some twenty barrels of bread and a few casks of water. Had we been wiser we should have sent more water, for we could not tell how distressed we might become for want of it on the shore if we did not find any spring of fair water on the island. However, I am recording what we did, and not what we ought to have done, and I can assure my friends that if ever they find themselves in such straits as we were in that night and day they will have reason to be thankful if they manage to keep all their wits about them, and to conduct their affairs with the same wisdom that they, as I make no doubt, display in less pressing hours. For myself, my wits were still wool-gathering, still were striving to remember something which for the life of me I could not manage to remember.

It was well-nigh evening, and twilight was making the distant land indistinct, when Hatchett came back from the last of those three voyages with very unpleasant tidings—that it was no use for us to send over any more provisions to the island, as those who had been disembarked there were only wasting that which they had already received. Indeed, Hatchett painted a gloomy picture of the conduct of those colonists who were now on shore, declaring that they had cast all discipline and decorum to the winds, and that they needed stern treatment if they were to be prevented from breaking out into open mutiny.

There were, of course, a great variety of folk among our colonists, and many of them were weak and foolish creatures enough, as there always will be weak and foolish creatures in any community of human beings until the human race grows into perfection, as some philosophers maintain that it will. Now, it certainly was precisely this element in our little society that had been shipped off to the island, for, with the women and children, it was the men who were most womanlike in their noise, or most childlike in their fears, whose safety we had first ensured. From what our Captain knew of these people, well-meaning enough under ordinary conditions, but timorous and foolish under conditions such as we now were in, he guessed that disorganisation and disturbance might be likely enough. Therefore he resolved, and his resolve was approved both by Hatchett and by Jensen, that he would go over himself to the island and restore order among the malcontents.

Now I will confess that when I heard of this my heart sank, for I took it for granted that Marjorie would go with Captain Marmaduke, and indeed it seemed only right that she should go rather than remain upon the Royal Christopher with only a parcel of rough men aboard her, and those rough men sorely divided in purpose, and each division mistrustful of the other. All through those long hours of shipwreck sorrow my spirits had been cheered by the sight of her beauty and the example of her calm. She weathered the calamity with the bravest temper; never cast down, never assuming a false elation, but bearing herself in all just as a true man would like the woman he loved to bear herself in stress and peril. I have read of a maid in France ages back who raised armies to drive my ancestors out of her fatherland and I think that maid must have looked as my maid did and had the same blessed grace to inspire courage and love and service.

So when I thought that Marjorie was about to quit the ship I felt such a sudden wrench at my heart as made me feel sick and dizzy, like a man about to faint. The water came into my eyes with the saltness of the sea, and words without meaning—words of pain, and grief, and longing—seemed to seek a form at my lips and then to perish without a breath. But at last, with an effort, I shook myself free of my stupor. I might never see her again, I told myself; this might be our latest parting, there on that wretched deck, in that crowd of faces painted with fear and fury, with the sullen sea about us which would so soon divide us. Come what might come of it, I swore that I would say my say and not carry the regret of a fool's silence to my grave. For though my heart seemed to beat like the drums of a dozen garrisons, I made my way across the slippery deck to where the girl stood, for the moment alone, with the wind flapping her hair about and blowing her gown against her. She was looking out at the island when I came close, and there was so much noise aboard and beyond that she did not hear my coming till I stood beside her, and called her name into her ear. Then she turned her pale face to me, and small blame to her to look pale in those terrors; but her eyes had all their brightness, and there was no sign of fear in them or on her lips. I thought her more beautiful than ever as she stood there, so calm in all that savage scene of ruin, so brave at a time when stout men shook with fear.

'Marjorie,' I said, 'I want to tell you something. I hope in God's mercy that we may meet again, but God alone knows if we ever shall. And so I want to tell you that, whatever happens to me, sick or well, in danger or out of it, I am your servant, and that your name will be in my heart to the end.'

She had heard me in quiet, but there was a wonder in her face as she listened to the words I stumbled over. In fear to be misunderstood, I spoke again in an agony.

'Marjorie,' I said, 'dear Marjorie, I should never have dared to tell you but for this hour. But I may never see you again, and I love you.'

And then I lost command of myself and my words, and begged her incoherently to forgive me, and to think kind thoughts of me if this were indeed farewell. She was silent for a moment, and there came no change over her face. Then she said softly:

'Why do you tell me this now? Is there some new danger?'

I stared at her in wonder.

'Marjorie,' I cried, 'Marjorie, are you not going to leave the ship?' She shook her head.

'I stay with Lancelot,' she answered quietly. 'It is an old promise between us. Where he is I abide. That is our compact.'

I cannot find any words for the fulness of joy that flooded my heart as Marjorie spoke. I would still be near her; the ruined ship remain a sacred dwelling. But in my error I had blundered, overbold, and I tried to explain confusedly.

'Marjorie,' I said, 'I thought you were going and I dared to tell you the truth. It is the truth indeed, but I should not have told it.'

She held out her hand to me with a kind smile as I clasped it.

'We are good friends,' she said. 'You and I and Lancelot. Let us remember nothing but that, that we are good friends, we three. I always think well of you; always deserve that I shall think well of you. Be always brave and good and God bless you!'

She let go my hand as she spoke and I turned away and left her, stirred by a thousand joys and fears and wonders.

By this time Captain Amber had made all his preparations, albeit with no small reluctance, to quit the ship. He picked out some ten of his men from those that had served him of old and that were now equipped as men of war. Then he formally entrusted to Lancelot the ship and the lives of all aboard her. Marjorie, who now came to him, he kissed very tenderly, making no attempt to urge her to accompany him. He knew the two so well and their love and loyalty each to the other. Then he took me by the hand and bade me serve Lancelot as I would serve him, which I faithfully and gladly promised to do, and so he went over the side into the skiff, with his men and Hatchett, and the sailors that were handling the skiff, and made his way towards the island.

It was now that a thing came to pass which relieved my mind of a care only to increase our anxieties. When the skiff was a little way from the ship my Captain, looking back to where we lay, drew from his pocket his kerchief, which was a big and brightly-coloured kerchief, such as men love who follow the sea, and waved it in our direction as a signal of farewell, and, no doubt, of encouragement. Now, I cannot quite tell the train of thought which the sight of that action aroused in my mind, but I think that it was something after this fashion. The waving of that kerchief reminded me of the waving of a flag, and the moment that the word flag came into my mind I suddenly remembered what it was that I had been trying to remember through all those weary hours. As in a mirror I saw again the interior of Jensen's cabin and the beautiful face of Barbara, smiling as she stooped over her hideous standard. I saw again that vile black flag, and as the picture painted itself upon my brain the consciousness of our peril came upon me in all its strength.

Without a doubt, the first thing to do was to tell Lancelot what I knew. It was too late now to tell the Captain. Even if he were not too far to see and understand such signals as we might make to him to return, it would not do to let Jensen and the rest of the crew know that we had fathomed their treachery. So I argued the matter to myself. It was certain that Jensen had no notion that I was any sharer in his dark secret, for though I could read in his face his dislike, I could see there no distrust of us. The first thing to be done was to break the bad news to Lancelot.

I drew Lancelot aside and told him what I had seen. At first he was amazed and incredulous; amazed because I had not warned Captain Amber before, and incredulous because, when I explained my forgetfulness through my fall and the hurt to my head, he would needs have it that I imagined the whole matter. But I was so confident in my tale that I shook his disbelief—at least, so far that he declared himself willing to take all possible precautions.

As matters stood we seemed to be in the better case. We had well-trained, well-armed men on our side; we had the supply of arms and ammunition in our care and under our guard; if the sailors were more numerous than we, they were practically unarmed. It was clear to both Lancelot and myself that the shipwreck, which had seemed so great a misfortune, was really the means of averting a more terrible calamity. We could not doubt that the intention of Jensen and his accomplices had been to seize the ship suddenly, taking us unawares when we were asleep, cutting most of our throats, very likely, and, after seizing upon the supply of arms, overawing such of the colonists and others as should be unwilling to convert the noble Royal Christopher into a pirate ship.

CHAPTER XX

A BAD NIGHT

Now our Captain had not been very long gone when the fair weather proved as fitful as a woman's mood, and the smiling skies grew sullen. That same moaning of the wind which we had heard with such terror on the preceding evening began to be heard again, and its sound struck a chill into all our hearts. The evening sky waxed darker, and the water that had been placable all day grew mutinous and mounted into waves—not very mighty waves, indeed, but big enough to make us all fearsome for the safety of our ship, for where the Royal Christopher was, perched upon that bank of ill omen, the force of the water was always greatest in any agitation, and there was ever present to our minds the chance that she might go to pieces before some sudden onslaught of the sea. In the face of that common peril we all forgot our watchfulness of each other, and Jensen and the sailors worked as earnestly to do all they could for the safety of our vessel as on our side Lancelot and I and the stout fellows under our command worked.

It was in all this trouble and hubbub that Marjorie showed herself to be the gallantest girl in the world. She was resolved to stay with Lancelot, but she was no less resolved to hamper him not at all by her presence. So when I came at dusk to the Captain's cabin to consult with Lancelot, who had shifted his quarters thither, I found his sister with him, but very changed in outward seeming. For she had slipped on a sea-suit of Lancelot's and her limbs were hid in a pair of seaman's boots and her fair hair coiled out of sight under a seaman's cap, and in this sea change she made the fairest lad in the world and might have been my Lancelot's brother to a hasty eye. She had a mind, she said, to play the man till fortune mended, and vowed to take her share of work with the best of us. At which Lancelot smiled sweetly and commended her wisdom in changing her rig, and as for me I would have adored her more than before, had that been possible, to find her so adaptable to danger. But there was little for her to do save to encourage us with her comradeship, and that she did bravely through it all, acting as any boy messmate might, and taking her place so naturally and simply in those hours of trial that it was not until later that I thought how strangely and how rarely she carried herself and how quietly she played her part.

"Her Fair Hair was Coiled Out of Sight Under a Seaman's Cap."

I shall never forget that terrible night on board the ship, with the waves smacking our poor sides, that groaned at every blow, and the wind moaning through the ruined rigging in a kind of sobbing way, as if all the elements were joining in a requiem for our foredoomed lives. There was never a moment when we could be sure that the next might not be our last; never a moment when we could not tell that the next wave might not sweep the ship with riven timbers into hopeless wreck, and plunge us poor wretches into the stormy seas to struggle for a few seconds desperately and unavailingly for our lives.

Through all that dismal night there was but little for us to do, and so I passed a portion of my time in the cabin fortifying my heart with the perusal of the book Mr. Davies gave me. I did not on that night neglect the thoughts of religion. Indeed, if I had been of a mind to, which Heaven be praised I was not, I could not have very well done so. For among our people there was a reverend man, one Mr. Ephraim Ebrow, whom extreme poverty had tempted to accompany Captain Amber's party, and this excellent man was at all times ready to deliver an exhortation, or to favour us with readings from the Holy Book. He was truly one of the Church Militant, and came of an old fanatique stock, and in moments of danger he was as gallant and as calm as any seasoned adventurer. He had a very fine voice, and it was no slight pleasure to hear him put up a prayer, or deliver a sermon, or read out chapters of the Scriptures in the authorised version. He himself, because he was no mean scholar, was wont to search the Scriptures from a Hebrew copy which he always carried with him. On this night he read to us many portions of the Scriptures, and got us to pray with him, and did many things of the kind that went to stay our alarm and strengthen our trust in the merciful wisdom of Providence. But that I found balm in the Holy Word was no reason why I should not find courage also from the plain words of a plain swordsman. So I read in my book by the light of a ship's lantern, and tried to give my thoughts to the exercise of weapons.

While I was reading thus in the cabin the door swung ajar, for ever since the accident the furniture of the ship was all put out of gear. Presently I heard the tramping of feet along the passage, and then the door was pushed open and Cornelys Jensen stood in the doorway and stared at me. I lifted my eyes and stared back at him.

'This is a wise way of passing the time,' he said with a sneer. 'Book-learning, forsooth, when the ship may go to pieces every instant.'

The tone of his voice galled me, and I answered him angrily, perchance rashly.

'I am no bookman,' I said. 'But there is nothing to do at this hour, and I feel no need for sleep.' For we had divided the night in watches, but I was wakeful as a hare that is being chased, and could not close my eyes to any purpose.

'Nay,' said I, 'there are worse things than reading a good book. Where is your black flag, Master Jensen?'

You should have seen how, just for a moment, he glared at me. He was armed, of course, and I think at that moment that he was sorely minded to take my life. But I had a pistol on the table, and my hand lay on the pistol, and the muzzle pointed across the table very straightly in the direction of Cornelys Jensen. Then the angry look fell away from his face, and he broke into long, low laughter, moving his head slowly up and down, and fixing me very keenly with his bright eyes.

'You are a smart lad,' he said at last. 'What the plague have you to do with my black flag?'

'What have you to do with it were a question more to the point,' I answered him, and I make no doubt now that in speaking as I did I was doing a very foolish thing. But I was only a boy, and inexperienced, and indeed all my life I have been given to blurting out things that mayhap I had better have kept to myself.

He laughed again.

'Nay,' he said, 'it is one of my most treasured possessions. I hauled it down with mine own hands from a pirate ship in my youth, when we captured the bark of that nefarious sea rover Captain Anthony. I have carried it with me for luck ever since, and it has always brought me luck—always till now.' Then he nodded his head again slowly twice or thrice. 'I will give it to you if you wish, Master Ralph,' he said; 'I will give it to you for luck.'

'I do not want it,' I said angrily, being somewhat confused with the turn things had taken. 'I am not superstitious for luck.'

Which indeed was not true, for I never met a seaman yet who was not superstitious; but I was wrathful, and I knew not what to say.

'Very well,' he said, 'very well. But you are welcome to it if you wish.'

Then he went out of the cabin without another word and drew the door behind him. I sat still for some seconds listening to the sound of his departing footstep.

Now I was bitterly vexed with myself. I had done a vain thing. I had put Jensen upon his guard by showing him that I knew something at least of his purposes, and I had put it into his power to offer a very ready explanation of suspicious circumstances. Indeed, how was I to know that what he said was not true? There was nothing whatever on the face of it unlikely, and if he told such a story to Captain Marmaduke, why, it was ten chances to one that Captain Marmaduke would implicitly believe in him. For there was no doubt about it, Captain Marmaduke had a great regard for Cornelys Jensen.

There was nothing for it but to tell Lancelot of what Jensen had said, and I did this with all dispatch. My statement had at least the effect of convincing Lancelot that I had in very fact seen what I had described to him about the flag. But I could see that Jensen's explanation had its effect upon him very much as I felt sure that it would have its effect upon Captain Marmaduke. Lancelot had nothing like the same regard for Jensen that his uncle had, but I knew that he did follow his uncle's lead in trusting him.

'You see, Ralph,' he said to me, 'this is a very likely story. Jensen is an old sailor. My uncle has told me a thousand times that he has served against pirates in his youth. What more natural than that he should preserve such a trophy of his prowess as the captured flag of some such villain as that same

84

Captain Anthony, of whom I have often heard? But we will be watchful none the less, and well on our guard.'

I could see that Lancelot did not share my fears as regarded Jensen, although he was troubled by the mutinous carriage of certain of the crew. I know that I was very apprehensive and unhappy, and that it seemed to me as if that night would never end.

CHAPTER XXI

RAFTS

When the day did break at last it brought no great degree of comfort with it. We were surrounded by a yellow, yeasty sea, and the air was so thick that the islands on which our lives depended seemed but shapeless shadows in the distance. Still the wind had abated somewhat, but the swell was very strong, and we were without any means of attempting to leave the vessel.

When it was quite morning, and the sky cleared a little, we saw the skiff, with the Captain on board, beating about on the water and trying to make for us. But in this he was not able to succeed, for the waves were running so high that it would have been quite impossible either to bring the skiff alongside or to get on board our vessel if he had done so. We could see the Captain standing up in the bows of the boat and signalling to us, and it made our hearts sick to be able to see him and to be unable to know what he wanted or what we ought to do.

At this moment one of the men—he was the ship's carpenter, and a decent, honest sort of fellow—said that he was a very good swimmer, and that he thought he could reach the skiff in that way. He was so very confident of his own powers that though we were somewhat unwilling to let him risk his life, he did in the end prevail upon Lancelot to let him make the attempt.

The man stripped and was into the sea in a moment, fighting bravely with the billows that buffeted him. It was a good sight to see him slowly forging his way through that yellow, clapping water; it is always a good sight to see a strong man or a brave man doing a daring thing for the sake of other people. We watched his body as he swam; he was but a common man, but his skin seemed as white as a woman's in that foul spume, and his black hair, which he wore long, streamed in a rail upon the water as a woman's might. But I do not think the woman ever lived who could swim as that man swam.

We watched him grow smaller and smaller, and most of us prayed for him silently as he fought his way through the waters. At last we saw that he had reached the skiff, and we could see that he was being pulled over the side. Then there came a long interval—oh, how long it seemed to us, as we watched the leaping waves and the distant skiff that leaped upon them, and wondered if the man's strength would carry him back again to us! By-and-by —it was not really such a very long time, but it seemed like centuries— Lancelot, who was looking through his spy-glass, said that the man was going over the skiff's side again. Then we all held our breaths and waited.

So it was; the fellow was swimming steadily back to us. It was plain enough to see that he was sorely fatigued, and that he was husbanding his strength, but every stroke that he gave was a steady stroke and a true stroke, and every stroke brought him a bit nearer to where we lay. And at last his black head was looking up at us beneath our hull, and in another second he had caught a rope and was on the deck again, dripping like a dog, and hard pushed for lack of breath.

Lancelot gave him a measure of rum with his own hands, and by-and-by his wind came back to him, and he found his voice to speak as he struggled into his clothes.

What he had to tell was not very cheering. He had given Captain Amber a faithful picture of our perils and our privations, and Captain Amber had made answer that he was sorry for us with all his heart, and only wished that he was in the danger with us. Which we knew very well to be true, though, indeed, the good gentleman was in scarcely less danger himself.

His orders to us were that we should with all speed construct rafts by tying together the planks of which we had abundance, and that we should embark upon these rafts and so try to make the shallop and the skiff, which would bear us in safety to the islands.

It was not tempting to make rafts and trust them and ourselves upon them to the sea that was churning and creaming beneath us, but it seemed to be well-nigh the only thing to do, and it was the Captain's orders, and we prepared to set to work and execute his commands. But we had scarce begun to tie a couple of planks together before it was plain that our labour would be in vain. For even while the man had been telling his tale the weather had grown much rougher, and we could see that the skiff was unable to remain longer near to us, but had to turn back for her own safety to the islands. I felt very sure that Captain Amber must be in anguish, having thus to leave us, his dear Lancelot and some seventy of his sailors and followers, on board a vessel that might cease to be a vessel at any moment.

Now we were in very desperate straits indeed, and some of us seemed tempted to give ourselves over to despair. If it had not been for the steadiness of those that were under Lancelot, I feel sure that the most part of the sailors would have paid no further heed to Jensen's counsels, but would have incontinently drunk themselves into stupor or madness, and so perished miserably.

But our men, if they were resigned to their fate, were resolved to meet it like Christians and stout fellows, and as we were the well-armed party the others had, sullenly enough, to fall in with our wishes. And Lancelot's wishes were that all hands should employ themselves still in the making of those rafts, so that if the weather did mend we should be able to take advantage of the improvement ere it shifted again. Though the water was beating up in great waves all about us, we were so tightly fixed upon our bank that we were well-nigh immovable, and it was possible for us to work pretty patiently and persistently through all the dirty weather. But though we worked hard and well, it took up the fag-end of that day and the whole of the next to get our two rafts ready for the sea, which was by that time more ready for them, as the storm had again abated.

CHAPTER XXII

WE LOSE CORNELYS JENSEN

It was on the night when we had well-nigh finished our two rafts that a very unexpected thing happened—a thing which I took at the time to be a piece of good fortune, but which, as it happened, proved to be a misfortune for some of us. The unexpected event was, namely, that we lost Cornelys Jensen; and this was the way in which the thing came about.

The nights during that spell of foul weather were very dark and moonless, not because there was no moon, though she was now waning into her last quarter, but because of the quantity of clouds that muffled up the face of the heavens and hid the moon and the stars from us. But we made shift as well as we could, working hard all the time that the daylight lasted, and giving up the night to the rest we were all in such sore need of. Of course, the usual discipline of the ship was preserved, the usual watches set, and all observed exactly as if Captain Amber himself had been aboard, for, though the Royal Christopher was sadly shaken, she was still uninjured as to her inward parts, and we were all able to sleep under cover and out of the way of wind or weather.

On the night before the weather mended, although it was not my watch and I was below in my cabin, I found that I could not sleep. The air was close and oppressive, full of a heat that heralded, though I did not know it, the coming of a spell of fine weather. I was feverish and distressed of body, and tossed for long enough in my hammock, trying very hard to get to sleep; but, though I was tired as a dog, the grace of sleep would not come to me. At last, in very desperation, I resolved to continue the struggle no longer. If I could not sleep I could not, and there was an end of it. I would go on deck and get there a little air to cool my hot body.

So up on deck I went and looked about me. All was quiet, all was dark. Here and there a ship's lanthorn made a star in the gloom; the ship seemed like a black rock rising out of blackness. I could hear the tread of the watch; I could hear the noisy lapping of the water. There was no wind, there was no moon; the air seemed to be thick and choking. I felt scarcely more refreshed than I had been in my cabin, but as I had come up I thought that I might as well stay up for a bit and have the benefit of whatever air there was. So I made my way cautiously in the darkness to the side of the vessel, and, leaning upon the bulwark, looked out over the sea, and fell to thinking of Marjorie and of my love for her and all its hopelessness.

Presently I heard voices. Those who spoke drew nearer and nearer to me, and I soon recognised the speakers as Lancelot and Cornelys Jensen. At the spot where I was standing a great pile of boxes and water barrels had been raised for transfer to the rafts, and I, being on the one side of this pile, was invisible to them as they approached, and would have been passed unnoticed had the night been brighter than it was. I could almost hear what they were saying; I am certain that I heard Jensen utter my name.

I came out of the shadow, or rather out of my corner—for it was all shadow alike—and called out Lancelot's name. Lancelot called back to me, and then I heard Jensen wish him good-night and turn and tramp heavily down the stairs that led below. He seemed to tramp very heavily, heavier than was his wont, for he was a light, alert man, even when his biggest sea-boots were on him, as I make no doubt they now were. Lancelot joined me, and I drew him with me into the place where I had been standing, after first casting a glance around the deck to see that no one was within hearing. All seemed deserted, save for the distant walk of the watch. We leaned over the bulwark together and began to talk.

I asked him what Jensen had been saying to him. He told me that Cornelys had come to him and expressed great surprise and anger at the doubts which he believed, from my manner and from some words that I had uttered, I entertained of him. It seemed that he had said again to Lancelot what he had said to me about the flag; that he insisted that there was no mystery at all about the matter, but that he was proud of its possession and superstitious as to its luck, and that he never was willingly parted from it. At the same time he offered to give it Lancelot, as he had already offered to give it me, if Lancelot was minded or wishful to take possession of it; an offer which Lancelot had refused.

I could see from Lancelot's manner that he was largely convinced of the integrity of Jensen, and I must confess that Jensen's conduct had given him grounds for confidence, and that I had very little in the way of reasonable argument to shake that confidence. Still, I made bold to be somewhat importunate with Lancelot. When he spoke of his uncle's trust in Jensen's integrity, when he urged the value of Jensen's services to us on the voyage, and the way in which he had kept the sailors under control at the first symptom of mutiny, I had, it must be confessed, little to say in reply that could seriously damage Jensen's character. But I was so thoroughly convinced of the man's treachery that I argued hotly, and it may be that as I grew hot I raised my voice a trifle, which is a way of mine; and, indeed, my voice is never a good whispering voice. I entreated Lancelot, at all events, to have a very watchful eye upon Jensen, and I urged that on the first symptom of anything in the least like double-dealing he should place Jensen under arrest.

Lancelot listened to me very patiently. He was impressed by my earnestness, and at last promised that he would scrutinise Jensen's actions very narrowly, and that if he saw anything that was at all suspicious in his demeanour he would immediately take steps to render him harmless. At this I pressed Lancelot's hand warmly, and was about to leave him and go below when I fancied that I heard steps stealing away from us very softly, from the other side of the pile of barrels and boxes by which we stood. I whipped out of my corner and round the pile in an instant, but there was no one there, and I could neither see nor hear anything suspicious. Lancelot declared that I was as suspicious as an old maid of her neighbour's hens. I echoed his laughter as well as I could, but I went below again with a heavy heart, for I was oppressed with a sense of danger which I dreaded the more because it seemed to lurk in darkness. I had laid me down again with no very great hope of sleep, but I had no sooner laid my head upon its pillow than I fell into a most uneasy slumber, in which all my apprehensions and all our perils seemed to be multiplied and magnified a hundredfold. A nightmare terror brooded upon my breast. Suddenly I imagined, in the swift changes of my dream, that we were sinking, and that the vessel was going to pieces with great crashes. I awoke with a start, to find that the noises of my dream were being continued into my waking life. The deck above was noisy with trampling feet and confused cries. For a moment I sat up, dizzy with surprise, and unable to realise whether I was awake or asleep. Then I pulled my wits together, and was on deck in a trice.

I caught hold of a sailor who was hurrying rapidly by, and asked him what was the matter. He answered me that there was a man overboard, and that they were doing all they could to save him by casting over the side spars and timbers that would float, in the hope that he might be able to catch one of them. The deck was all confusion, men running hither and thither, and some hanging over the bulwarks and peering into the darkness, in the vain hope of catching a glimpse of their drowning comrade. We had not a boat to lower, save only the little dinghy, which would not have lived a minute in such a sea.

When I found somebody who could tell me what had happened this was what I learnt. A man had fallen overboard; the watch had heard the splash as the body fell into the water, and a wild cry that followed upon the splash; a sailor had shouted out his warning of 'Man overboard!' and the cry had roused the whole ship. Up to this point nobody seemed to have any idea who the missing man was, but when Lancelot, who was immediately on deck, though he had but just gone to lie down, had commanded silence, and the men were gathered about him on the deck, the sailor who had first made the alarm was found and questioned. This sailor said that he saw a man standing at the vessel's side at a place where, when the mast fell, the bulwark had been torn away and had left a gaping wound in the ship's railings; that as he, surprised at seeing a man there, came nearer to try and ascertain what he was doing, the man staggered, flung up his arms—here the man who was narrating these things to us flung up his hands in imitation—and then went over the side with a great splash and a great cry. He believed that the man was none other than Cornelys Jensen.

When Lancelot and I heard the name of Cornelys Jensen upon the man's lips we looked involuntarily at each other, and I make certain that we both grew pale. That the man of whom we had been talking not an hour before in such different terms should have thus suddenly been taken out of our lives came like a shock to us both. Further investigation confirmed the accuracy of the man's statement. The roll was called over, and every man answered to his name except Cornelys Jensen. His cabin was at once searched, but he was not in it, and it was evident that he had made no attempt to sleep there that night, for his hammock was undisturbed. On the table lay a folded sheet of paper, which Lancelot took up and opened. It contained only these words: 'Your doubts have driven me to despair.' These words had apparently been followed by some other words, the beginning of a fresh sentence, but, whatever they were, they were so scrawled over with the pen that their meaning was as effectually blotted out as if they had never been written.

Of course, all efforts to rescue the unhappy man were unavailing. There was really nothing that we could do save to cast pieces of spar and plank overboard in the faint hope that some one of them might come in the drowning man's way and enable him to keep afloat till daylight, if by any chance his purpose of self-slaughter—for so it seemed to me—had changed with his souse into the water. The night was pitchy black, and the waves were running a tremendous pace, so that there really seemed to be little likelihood of the strongest swimmer keeping himself long afloat; but we did our best and hoped our hardest, even those of us who, like myself, disliked and distrusted Cornelys Jensen profoundly.

Though Lancelot said little to Marjorie beyond the bare news of what had happened I could see that he took the disappearance of Jensen and that little scrawl we found in his cabin badly to heart. He was convinced at once that Jensen had committed suicide, driven thereto by the suspicions that we had formed of him; and, indeed, though I tried to console Lancelot as well as I could, it did look very like it, and I must confess that I felt a little guilty. For though I still thought that the grounds upon which I had formed my suspicions of the man were reasonable grounds, and justified all my apprehensions, still I could not resist an uncomfortable feeling that perhaps, after all, I might have misjudged the man, and that in any case I was the instrument—the unwitting instrument, but still the instrument none the less—of sending a fellow-creature before his Maker with the stigma of self-slaughter upon his soul. So certainly Lancelot and I passed a very unhappy night, what there was left of it; and when the dawn came we scanned the sea anxiously in the faint hope that we might see something of the missing man. But, though the sea was far quieter than it had been for many hours, there was no trace of any floating body upon it, and it became only too clear to our minds that, for some cause or other, Cornelys Jensen had indeed killed himself. I could only imagine that the man was really crazed, although we did not dream of such a thing, and that the perils and privations through which we had passed, and against which he seemed to bear such a bold front, had in fact completed the unhinging of his wits, and that my accusations, acting upon a weakened mind, had driven him in his frenzy to destroy himself. To be quite candid, though I was sufficiently sorry for the man, I was still dogged enough in my own opinion of his character as to think that, if it was the will of Providence that he should so perish, at all events the Royal Christopher was no loser by his loss.

CHAPTER XXIII

WE GET TO THE ISLAND

Even if we had lost a better man than Jensen it would have been our duty none the less to work hard the next day to get our rafts ready and fit for sea. Very few men are indispensable to their fellows, and certainly, as far as making the rafts was concerned, it would have been far more serious if Abraham Janes, the carpenter, had taken it into his head to throw himself overboard than that Cornelys Jensen had taken it into his head to do so. Yet, in a manner, too, we missed Cornelys Jensen. He was an able man, full of all kinds of knowledge, and he had a domineering way with the seamen which they seemed to recognise and to obey unflinchingly. These fellows, for the most part, took the tidings of his death very indifferently. Some of them seemed to miss him as a trained dog might miss his master. Some, again, seemed scarcely to miss him at all. One or two, and especially the fellow who saw the death and the manner of it, seemed to take the matter very greatly to heart, and to go about with a sad brow and a sullen eye in consequence.

As for Lancelot and myself, I must say that we soon grew to accept his loss with composure. There was so much to do that there would have been little time for a greater grief than either of us could honestly wear. The weather was mending hourly, and the rafts were making rapid progress. By the end of that day they were finished and ready for the sea.

By this time, so strange are the chops and changes of the weather in that part of the world, the sea and sky were as gentle as on a summer's day. I have heard the phrase 'as smooth as a mill-pond' applied to salt water many a thousand times, but never, indeed, with so much truth as if it had been applied to the ocean that day. It lay all around us, one tranquillity of blue, and above it the heavens were domed with an azure fretted here and there with fleeces of clouds, even as the water was fretted here and there with laces of foam. In the clear air we could see the islands ahead of us sharply dark against the sky, and as we watched them our longing to be at them, to tread dry land again, was so great as to be almost unbearable. Those who have lived on shore all their lives can form little or no idea of the way in which the thoughts of a man who is tasting the terrors of shipwreck for the first time turn to a visible land, and how they burn within him for longing to walk upon turf or highway once again in his jeopardised life.

Now, the rafts that we had constructed were by no means ill-fashioned. That ship's carpenter, Abraham Janes, was a man of great parts in his trade. I never in my life saw a handier man at his tools or a defter at devices of all kinds. The poor old Royal Christopher had timber enough and to spare for the planks that were to make our rafts, and we had a great plenty of idle rope aboard in the rigging wherewith our fallen mast was entangled. So there was no lack of material, and when our men saw that there was really and truly a prospect of escape there was no lack of willing hands to work. So by the end of the time I have already specified we had two large and serviceable rafts ready to try their fortunes upon the ocean that was now so tempting in its calm.

It was a matter of some little surprise to us who were on board the ship that with the calm weather Captain Amber made no further attempt to come out to us. But there was no sign of a sail upon the water, although we watched it eagerly through the spy-glass; and we were sorely puzzled to imagine what could have happened to our leader, for that he could be forgetful of or indifferent to our danger it was impossible to believe.

The rafts being now ready and the weather so propitious, nothing was left for us but to commit them, with ourselves and all our belongings, to the water, in the hope of making the shore with them. They were each of them capable of holding our whole number and a quantity of such stores as were left on board. These latter, therefore, divided into two equal parts, we proceeded to put upon the rafts as quickly as we could, together with as many barrels of water as we had. Each of the rafts carried a stout mast and sail, and in the absence of any wind could be propelled slowly over such a smooth water as that which now lay around us by means of oars. The stores and water barrels we adjusted in such a way as to preserve as nicely as might be the balance of the rafts.

We effected the transfer of our stores and provisions with very little difficulty, and embarked all our party, also without any difficulty whatever. In obedience to Lancelot's resolution, which he had privately communicated to me beforehand, we divided our forces into two parties. That is to say, half of the sailors were set on each raft, and with each raft half of our armed men; for though we had little or no apprehension now that there would be any trouble with the sailors, we still deemed it best to let them see very plainly that we were and meant to be the masters. I went on the one raft, Lancelot—and of course Marjorie with him—upon the other, and when all was ready we pushed away from the Royal Christopher and trusted ourselves and our fortunes to our new equipages.

There was happily little danger, even little difficulty, about the enterprise. The rafts were well made; they rode on the waters like corks. What little wind there was blew towards the islands, and the sea was as placid as a lake, so that the men could use their big oars easily enough. It was indeed slow work to paddle these great rafts along, but it was quite unadventurous, so that I have little or nothing to record of note concerning our journey. Little by little the Royal Christopher grew smaller and smaller behind us, with her great mast sticking out so sadly over her side; little by little the island loomed larger and larger on our view. At last, after a couple of hours that were the most pleasurable we had passed for many days, we came close to the island, and could see that the colonists were all crowded together upon the beach, waiting to receive us.

The island was very large, rocky, and thickly wooded, and the coast was rocky too, and the water very shoaly, which made me understand how difficult landing must have been in the stormy weather. But now, with the sea so fair and the weather so fine, we had little or no difficulty in getting ashore, and with the eager assistance of the colonists were soon able to effect the landing of all our stores and belongings.

Our first great surprise on our arrival was to see no sight of Captain Amber amongst those who were gathered upon the beach to receive us. But his absence was soon explained in reply to our anxious inquiries. It seemed that a great spirit of discontent prevailed among the colonists upon that island, and that they upbraided Captain Amber very bitterly for being the cause of their misfortunes: as is the way with weak-spirited creatures, who have not the heart to bear a common misfortune courageously. To make a long story short, they insisted that he must needs endeavour to find some means of rescue for them by getting into the sea track and persuading some ship to come to their aid and take them from the island; which certainly was a disconsolate place enough, especially for people who were always ready to make a poor mouth over everything that did not please them. As the sailors who were with Captain Amber sided with the colonists in this matter, he had no choice but to consent; and as his vessel was fairly sea-worthy, he and his people had departed, in the hope of meeting some ship to bring all succour. Captain Marmaduke was, it seems, most loath to depart while we were in such a plight on board of the Royal Christopher; but there was no help for it, for his men were almost in open mutiny, and would have carried him on board would he or no. So he had sailed away and the colonists were all hopeful, in their silly, simple way, that he would soon return in a great ship and carry them to a land as lovely as a dream, where all their wishes would be fulfilled for the asking, and where each man would have his bellyful of good things without the working for it. For that was, it seems, the notion most of these fellows had in their heads of poor Captain Amber's Utopia.

I had begun to perceive by this time that a very large number of those that had come out with Captain Amber aboard of the Royal Christopher were but weak-spirited creatures, and such as might be called fair-weather friends. So long as all was going well and there was a prospect before them of a prosperous future and everything they wanted, they were supple enough and loud to laud the good gentleman who was conveying them to comfort. But with the break in our luck their praises and their patience went in a whiff, and they showed themselves to be such a parcel of wrong-headed, grumbling, disheartened and dispiriting knaves as ever helped to shake a good man's courage. They were as ready to imprecate Captain Amber now as they had been to load him with praises before, and in this they were supported by all the worser sort—and these were the greater part—among the sailors that had stayed with the colonists. But with Lancelot's arrival upon the island he soon put a stop to all loudly expressed grumbling—or at least to all grumbling that was loudly expressed in his hearing. There were some good fellows amongst the colonists, and the old soldiers were staunch and sturdy fellows, who adored Captain Amber, and Lancelot after him. So, as we had these with us, we made the grumblers keep civil tongues in their heads, aye and work too to the bettering of our conditions. The first party had made themselves some huts and now we made more for ourselves who were new-comers, with tents of a kind out of sail-cloth that we had brought from the ship, and for Lancelot a large double hut covered with some of this same cloth for him and Marjorie to dwell in. And, Lord! what a joy it was to see how Marjorie bestirred herself making herself as good a lieutenant to Lancelot as Captain's heart could desire. But we were all so busy that in those hours on that island I seldom had speech with her, for my care was chiefly with those discontented and weaklings who were so eager to complain and make mischief.

It seemed to me then that the best man of all that pack was the woman Barbara Hatchett. For while the colonists were making poor mouths over their plight and piping as querulously as sparrows after rain, and while the sailors were for the most part sour and sullen, Barbara took her lot with cheerfulness, and had smiles and smooth words for everybody and everything. She had even smiles and smooth words with me, who had exchanged no speech with her beyond forced greeting for this many a day. For she came up to me laughing once, at a time when I stood alone and was, indeed, thinking of Marjorie who was busy in her hut at some task that Lancelot had set her. Barbara began to banter with me in a way that seemed strange with her, saying that I was fickle like all my sex, that I was sighing for fair hair now, who had doted on black locks a few years ago, and much more idle talk to the same want of purpose. At last she asked me bluntly if I had loved her once, and when I answered yes, she asked me if I loved her still, now that she was a married woman; and without giving me time to answer she said that she had a kindness for me, and would do me a good turn yet for the sake of old days when she came to be queen.

I was vexed with her for the vanity and importunity of her mirth, and to stop her words I asked her bluntly if she had ever seen a black flag. But my question had no effect to disconcert her gaiety.

'You mean the black flag of poor Jensen?' she said; and when I nodded she began to pity Jensen for his belief in his trophy, which, after all, had brought him no more luck than a sea grave; and then she went on with shrillish laughter to tell me that she had begged it of him to give her to make into a petticoat, 'For it would have made a bonny petticoat, would it not?' she said suddenly, coming to a sharp end and looking me earnestly in the face.

I was at a loss what to say, being so flustered by her carriage and her words, which seemed to make it plain to me that I had sorely misjudged the dead man. But I said nothing, and moved a little way from her; and she, seeing my disinclination, laughed again, and then 'God blessed' me with a vehemence and earnestness that, as I thought, meant me more harm than good. But after that she turned and went back to the rest of the women, and I could see her going from one to the other, soothing and comforting them, and showing them how to make the best of their bitter commons on the island. And as I watched her I wondered; but I had little time for watching or for wondering.

CHAPTER XXIV

FAIR ISLAND

For the nonce I will make bold to leave Captain Marmaduke sailing the seas and to occupy myself solely with the fate of those who were encamped on the island, and chiefly of Marjorie and Lancelot and thereby myself who had the good fortune to be with them to the end of the enterprise. And, oh, as I think of Marjorie in those days it is ever with fresh wonder and delight and infinite gratitude to Heaven for the privilege to have seen her. She seemed just a boy with boys, she with Lancelot and me, and she wore her boyish weed with a simple straightforward ease that made it somehow seem the most right and natural thing in the world. But that was ever her way; whatever she did seemed fit and good, and that not merely to my eyes who loved her, but, as I think, to most. And she was very helpful in mind and body, always eager to bear her share in any work that was toward, and in council advising wisely without assertion. It might seem at first blush a handicap for adventurers to have a girl on their hands, but we did not find it so, only always, save for the peril in which the maid was, a gain and blessing. And so to our fortunes. You must know that from the further coast of our island—the further from our wreck, I mean—we could discern the outlines of other islands, the nearest of which appeared to be within but a few hours' sail. It was plain, therefore, that we were, very fortunately for us, cast away in the neighbourhood of a considerable archipelago, and that we had every reason on the whole to rejoice at our condition instead of bewailing it.

Now, though the island we were on was in many ways fair and commodious, we were not without confidence that another island, which lay a little further off, as it might be a couple of hours' sail, would serve us even in better stead, and at least we resolved to explore it. So Lancelot and Marjorie and I, with some thirty of our own men, resolved to cross over in the shallop boat which had conveyed the first party to the island while the weather was still fair, taking with us a great plenty of arms and implements, canvas and abundance of provisions, as well as a quantity of lights and fireworks, which we had saved from the ship, and which Lancelot thought might be useful for many purposes. It was agreed between us and the colonists that if we found the new island better than the old we were to make great bonfires, the smoke of which could not fail to be seen from the first island, or Early Island, as we came to call it. This they should take as a signal to come with all speed to the new camping-ground.

You must not think it strange that we set out upon this expedition thoughtlessly and leaving the other folk unprotected. For, in the first place, there were a goodly number of the colonists—as many in number as the sailors; and, in the second place, the sailors were not so well-armed as many of the colonists were, having nothing but their knives and a few axes. Furthermore, as Cornelys Jensen was not among them, and as it seemed most unlikely that the purpose, if purpose he had, would hold with his fellows now that there was, as it were, no ship to seize, we felt that there could be no danger to our companions in leaving them while we went on our voyage of exploration. So you will please to bear in mind how matters now stood. There was Captain Marmaduke in the skiff, who had sailed away from us to seek succour for us all. There was on the island with which we had first made acquaintance the majority of our colonists—men, women and children, together with the greater part of the sailors—under the authority of Hatchett. There were, further, Lancelot and Marjorie and myself and our thirty men, who had gone off in the shallop to explore the adjacent islands in the hope of finding a better resting-place for our whole party. As for Cornelys Jensen, I took him to be at the bottom of the sea.

We had arranged that during our absence the administration of the colony should be vested in a council, of whom the Reverend Mr. Ebrow was one and Hatchett another, for, as the leading man among sailors, he could not be overlooked, and I mistrusted him no more now that Jensen was gone. Certain of the soldierly men and two or three of the most cool-headed amongst the colonists made up the total of this council, whose only task would be to apportion the fair share of labour to each man in making the island as habitable a place as might be till our return. For, after all, it was by no means certain that we should have better luck with the near island, and in any case it was well to be prepared for all emergencies.

It was late on the second day of our arrival at the island that Lancelot and Marjorie and I with our companions set off on our expedition. We followed the coast-line of our island a long while, keeping a sufficiently wide berth for fear of the shoals. When we had half circumnavigated it there lay ahead of us the island for which we were making. It lay a good way off, and, as the day was very fine and still, it seemed nearer to us than it proved to be. As far as we could judge at that distance, it seemed to be a very much larger island than the one which we had just left; and so indeed it proved to be.

The shallop was a serviceable vessel, and ran bravely before the wind on the calm sea. Had the wind been fully in our favour we should have made the island for which we were steering within the hour; but it blew slightly across our course, compelling us to tack and change our course often, so that it was a good two hours before we were close to our goal. When we came close enough we saw that the island seemed in all respects to be a more delectable spot than that island on which chance had first cast us. There was a fine natural bay, with a strand of a fine, white, and sparkling sand such as recalled to me the aspect of many of the little bays and creeks in the coast beyond Sendennis, and in the recollection brought the tears into my mouth, not into my eyes. From this strand we could see that the land ran up in a gentle elevation that was very thickly wooded. Beyond this again rose in undulating succession several high hills, that might almost be regarded as little mountains, and these also seemed to be densely clothed with trees. Marjorie declared that the place looked in its soft greenness and the clean whiteness of its shore a kind of Earthly Paradise, and indeed our hearts went out to it. I found afterwards, from conversation with my companions, that every man of us felt convinced on our first close sight of Fair Island, as we afterwards called it, that we should find there abundance of water and all things that we needed which could reasonably be hoped for.

We came, after a little coasting, to a small and sheltered creek, into which it was quite easy to carry our vessel. The creek ran some little way inland, with deep water for some distance, so here we beached the shallop and got off and looked about us.

Although by this time the day was grown somewhat old, we were determined to do at least a measure of exploring then and there, and ascertain some, at least, of the resources of our new territory. There was, of course, the possibility that we might meet with wild animals or with still wilder savages, but we did not feel very much alarm about either possibility. For we were a fairly large party; we were all well-armed, and well capable of using our weapons. Each of us carried pistols and a hanger, Marjorie with the rest, she being as skilful in their use as any lad of her age might be. For my own part I always wore in my coat pocket a little pistol Lancelot had given me, that looked like a toy, but was a marvel of mechanism and precision. Weaponed as we were, we had come, moreover, into that kind of confidence which comes to those who have just passed unscathed through grave peril, a confidence which is, as it were, a second wind of courage.

It would not do, of course, to leave our boat unprotected, so it was necessary to tell off by lot a certain number of our men to stay with it and guard it. All the men were so eager for exploration that those upon whom the lots fell to remain behind with the shallop made rather wry faces; but Lancelot cheered them by telling them that theirs was a position to the full as honourable as that of explorers, and that in any case those who looked after the boat one day should be relieved and go with the exploring party on the next day, turn and turn about.

This satisfied them, and they settled down to their duty in content. It was agreed upon that in case of any danger or any attack, whether by savages or by wild beasts—for in those parts of the world there might well be monstrous and warlike creatures—they were to make an alarm by blowing upon a horn which we had with us, and by firing a shot. It was to be their task while we were away to prepare a fire for our evening meal. We had our supply of provisions and of water with us, but those of us who were to explore had very good hopes that we should bring back to the skiff not merely the good news that we had found water, but also something in the way of food for our supper. Lancelot, for one, expressed his confidence that there must be game of various kinds in so thickly a wooded place, and when Lancelot expressed an opinion I and the others with me always listened to it like Gospel.

Luckily for us, we soon found one and then another spring of fresh water. But it took us a matter of three days to explore that island thoroughly, for it was very hilly, and in many parts the woods were well-nigh impenetrable in spite of our axes. Most of the trees and shrubs had at this time either blossoms or berries on them, red, white, and yellow, that filled the air with sweet and pungent odours. It was a large island, and on the other side of the ridge of hills which rose up so sharply from the place where we first landed the land stretched almost level for a considerable distance before it dropped again in low cliffs to the sea. Part of this plain was grass-grown land, not unlike English down land, but in other parts the grass grew in great tufts as big as a bush, intermixed with much heath, such as we have on our commons in England; part of it was thickly grown with all manner of bright flowers and creeping plants, that knotted themselves together in such an entanglement that it was very hard to cut a path. We had need to go carefully here, for suspicion of snakes. We found no sign of savage wild beasts, though of harmless ones there were plenty, some of which made very good meat. As for savages, we saw none; and as far as we could make out we were the only human beings upon the island. Yet Lancelot, who was wonderfully quick at noting things, thought that he detected signs here and there which went to show that we were not the first men who had ever explored it. There were few land fowls—only eagles of the larger sort, but five or six sorts of small birds. There were waterfowl in abundance of many varieties, with shellfish to our hands, and good fish for the fishing, so between the sea and the land we were in no fear of want of victual, which cheered us very greatly.

We had rigged up some rough tents with our canvas, one apart for Marjorie and one for me and Lancelot, and half a dozen for our men, and altogether our condition had fair show of comfort, and to me indeed seemed full of felicity.

Until we had thoroughly explored the island we did not deem it wise to make our promised communication with the former island. But as soon as we had pretty well seen all that there was to be seen, we thought that, the time still being fair, we could scarcely do better than get our fellow-adventurers over. Our men were therefore set to work collecting as large a quantity of fuel as might be, and in clearing a path to the summit of the nearest hill, from which we might set off our bonfire to the best advantage.

Our men were all dispersed about the island busy at this business, and Marjorie was in her tent, taking at her brother's entreaty the rest she would never have allowed herself. It was a very hot day, and Lancelot and I, who had been collecting firewood on the near slope of the hill, but a few yards from the creek where our craft was beached, were lying down for a brief rest under a tree and talking together of old times. The sight of a small gaudy parrot, of which there was an abundance in the island, had sent our memories back to that parlour of Mr. Davies's where we had first met, and where there were parrots on the wall, and so we chatted very pleasantly.

By-and-by our talk flagged a little, for we grew drowsy with the heat, and our eyes closed and we fell into dozes, from which we would lazily wake up to enjoy the warm air and the bright sunlight and the vivid colours of everything about us, sea and sky and trees and flowers and grasses.

I remember very well musing as I lay there upon the strangeness of disposition which leads men to pine out their lives in the mean air of smoky cities, with all their hardship and their unloveliness, when the world has so many brave places only waiting for bold spirits to come and dwell therein. Boylike, I had forgotten all the perils which I had undergone before ever I came to Fair Island. I was only conscious of the delicious appearance of the place, of our good fortune in finding so fair a haven; and if only Captain Marmaduke and my mother had been with us I think I could have been very well content to pass the remainder of my days upon that island, which seemed to me to the full as enchanted as any I had read of in the Arabian tales.

I had dropped into a kind of sleep, in which I dreamt that I was Sindbad the Sailor, when I was awakened by a light step and the sound of a soft voice. I looked up and saw that Marjorie was bending over Lancelot, who was sitting up by me. She held him by the arm and pointed out across the sea.

'Don't you see something out there?' she asked, speaking quite low, as she always did when excited by anything.

Lancelot and I followed the direction of her gaze and her outstretched finger, and discerned very far away upon the sea a small black object. It lay between us and the island we had left, but somewhat to the right of it.

'What is it?' I asked.

'That's just what I want to know,' said Marjorie. 'How if it should be savages?'

The very thought was disquieting. We had grown so secure that we had almost forgotten the possibility of such dangers; but now, at Marjorie's words, the possibilities came clearly back to me. Captain Marmaduke had told us many a time stories about savages and their war canoes and their barbarous weapons, and it was very likely indeed that what we saw was a boat filled with such creatures creeping across the sea to attack us.

It moved very slowly across the smooth waters, and there was a strong bright sun, which played upon the surface of the water very dazzlingly, which added to our difficulty in understanding the floating object. But as it came slowly nearer we saw that it must be some kind of vessel, for we distinguished what was clearly a mast with a sail, though, as there was very little wind that morning, the sail hung idly by the mast. A little later we were able to be sure that what we saw was a kind of raft, with, as I have said, a mast and sail, but that its propulsion came from some human beings who were aboard it, and who were causing its slow progress with oars. By this time I had got out a spy-glass from our tent; and then Lancelot gave a cry of amazement, for he recognised in the new-comers certain of those colonists our companions whom we had left behind on the hither island. There were five of them on board, all of whom Lancelot named to us, and as he named them, Marjorie and I, looking through the glass in turns, were able to recognise them too. By-and-by they saw us too, for one of them stood up on the raft, and stripping off his shirt waved it feebly in the air as a signal to us, a signal which we immediately answered by waving our kerchiefs. It takes a long time to tell, but the thing itself took longer to happen, for it must have been fully an hour after we first noted the raft before it came close to the shore of our island.

As soon as it was within a couple of boats' lengths Lancelot and I, in our impatience and our anxiety to aid, ran into the water, which was shallow there, for the beach sloped gently, and was not waist high when we reached the voyagers, so that we had no fear of sharks. The new-comers were huddled together on as rudely fashioned a raft as it had ever been my lot to see, and had it not been for the astonishing tranquillity of the sea it is hard to believe that they could have made a hundred yards without coming to pieces. They all leaped into the water now, and between us we ran the crazy raft on to the beach, Lancelot and I doing the most part of the work, for the poor wretches that had been on board of her seemed to be sorely exhausted and scarcely able to speak as they splashed and staggered through the shallow water to the shore, where Marjorie was waiting anxiously for us.

They did speak, however, when once they were safely on dry land and had taken each a sip from our water-bottles, for all their throats were parched and swollen with thirst. It was a terrible tale which they had to tell, and it made us shiver and grow sick while they told it. I will tell it again now, not, indeed, in their words, which were wild, rambling, and disconnected, but in my own words, making as plain a tale of it as I can, for indeed it needs no skill to exaggerate the horror of it.

CHAPTER XXV

THE STORY FROM THE SEA

In few words, it came to this. The sailors on the island had proved themselves to be as bloody villains as had ever fed the gallows. They had taken the unhappy colonists by surprise and had massacred them, all but the women and the children. As for the women—poor things!—it would have been better for them if they had been killed with the others, but their lives were spared for greater sorrows. Those who told us that tale were all that were left, they said, of the unhappy company. They had escaped by mere chance to the woods, and had fashioned with their axes the rough raft and oars which had conducted them at last to us and to temporary safety.

This was their first raw story. Horrid as it was it took a stronger horror when one of the men shouted a curse at Cornelys Jensen.

'Cornelys Jensen!' I cried. 'Cornelys Jensen—Cornelys Jensen is dead, and the seas have swallowed him.'

The man who had uttered his name gave a great groan.

'Would to Heaven they had,' he said. 'But Heaven has not been so merciful. That tiger still lives and lusts for blood.'

Marjorie and Lancelot and I glanced at each other in amazement, and the same thought crossed all our minds—that fear and grief had crazed the unhappy man who was speaking to us. But he, reading something of our thoughts in our eyes, turned to his fellows for confirmation, and confirmation they readily gave. Cornelys Jensen was alive. Cornelys Jensen was on the island. Cornelys Jensen was the instigator of the massacre, the bloodiest actor in the bloody work.

Here was indeed amazing tidings, and we cried to know more, but the men had no more to tell. They had no knowledge of how Cornelys Jensen made his appearance upon the island; all they knew was that he did appear, and that his appearance was the signal for a display of weapons on the part of the sailors on his side and the massacre of all the unhappy wretches who were not inclined to his piratical purposes. The colonists seemed to have made no sort of stand for their lives. Indeed, it would appear that they were taken quite unawares, and that the most were struck down before they had time to act in their own defence. As for the miserable wretches who told us this tale, they had fled to the woods when the wicked business began, and the murderers

106

either lost count of them or imagined that they must perish miserably of famine in the forest. Indeed, they must have so perished if it had not occurred to one of them, who had his wits a little more about him than the others, to suggest the manufacture of a raft, whereby they might make the attempt to reach the island, where, as they guessed, we, with our well-armed fellows, were safely settled. 'For,' as the man argued, 'we risk death either way. If we stop here we must either perish among these trees for lack of sustenance or must creep back to the piratical camp with little other hope than a stroke from a hanger, or tempt the seas in the hope of friends and safety.' So they fashioned a raft as well as they could out of a number of fallen trees, which they fastened together with natural ropes made of the long creeping plants that abounded, and that were as tough and as endurable as ever was rope that was weaved out of honest hemp. They found enough timber for their craft among the fallen tree trunks, and they had the less difficulty in their work that one of their number was Janes, who had his saw in his belt at the moment of their flight to the woods.

Long before they finished telling their tale our men, who were scattered abroad in the woods, came tumbling down to us at the sound of the horn, that Lancelot wound to summon them, and gathered in horror around their unhappy comrades. As for me, I was so amazed at the news that Cornelys Jensen was alive that I stood for awhile like one stunned, and could say nothing, but only stare at those pale faces and wonder dumbly. When after awhile the power of speech did return to me I strove with many questions to find out how Jensen was thus restored to life and to evil deeds, but as to that they none of them knew anything. If the marvel of Jensen's reappearance was the greatest marvel, marvel only second to it was how the sailors who obeyed him came to have weapons for their business. As to that, again, the fugitives could give no help. The sailors had arms, every man of them, muskets and pistols and cutlasses, and had used them with deadly effect. It was all a mystery that made our senses sick to think upon.

Of one thing the fugitives were very positive—that Jensen and his murderers would very soon make a descent upon our island, in the hope of surprising us unawares and killing us. For now they were very numerous, and at least as well-armed as we were, and would make very formidable enemies. The only wonder was that they had not already attempted it, but the men believed that the villains were so engrossed in a swinish orgie after their triumph as to be heedless of time or prudence. So here were we—but thirty-two men in all, not counting these fugitives—and with one woman, though so brave an one—in urgent peril. It was fortunate for us all that in Lancelot's youth there was an alliance of courage with skill which would have done credit to a general of fifty. I was not much in those days in the way of giving advice, but I was strong and active, and ready to obey Lancelot in all things, which was what was most wanted of me in that juncture. We had every reason to be confident in the fidelity and courage of the men who were with us, and our confidence was not misplaced.

The first thing to be done was to settle the fugitives in the utmost comfort we could afford them. We put them to rest in one of our tents we had built, and gave to each of them a taste of strong waters, after which we urged them to sleep if they could, adding, to encourage them in that effort, that the sooner their bodies were refreshed by rest and food the better they would be able to bear their part in resisting the common enemy. This argument had great weight with the men, who were very willing to be of help, but too hopelessly worn out just then to be of the smallest aid to us or the smallest obstacle to our enemies. Indeed, the poor fellows were so broken with fear and suffering that I think they would have slept if they had heard that Cornelys Jensen, with all his pack, had landed upon the island. As it was, in a very few minutes all of them were lying in a row and sleeping soundly. I could almost have wept as I looked upon them lying there so quiet and so miserable, and thought of all the high hopes with which they had entered upon the adventure that had proved so disastrous for them and so fatal for so many of their companions.

Having thus disposed of them, our next course was to take such steps as we could towards strengthening our position. To begin with, we hauled our boat further up the creek than she now was, for it would be a terrible misfortune to us if anything were to happen to her, seeing that on her depended any chance we had of leaving the island if we were so far pushed as to have to make the attempt. Our position was not an easy one to attack as it stood, coming, as the attack must, from the island we had left, for of an attack in our rear we had no danger. Even if Cornelys Jensen were able to get to the back of our island, it would take him an intolerable time to make his way through the well-nigh impenetrable woods that lay between us. On our front we felt confident that the attack would come, and we felt further confident that, even if it was made with the full force of ruffians that Jensen had at his command, we ought to be able to repulse it, and to prevent the scoundrels from effecting a landing. For though the news that they were thoroughly equipped with the weapons and munitions of war was wofully disheartening news, still, as we were well-armed ourselves, it did not altogether discourage us. They might be very well two to one, but two to one is no such great odds when the larger party has to effect a landing upon an open place held by resolute men and well weaponed.

It was, in Lancelot's judgment, our first duty to erect a sort of fort or stockade upon the beach, wherein we could take shelter if we were really hard pressed, and wherein we could store for greater safety our stores and ammunition from our skiff. We had set up several huts along the shore of the creek for habitation and for storage of our goods. But they would have offered no protection in case of an attack, being but mere shells hurriedly put together, and intended merely as temporary shelters from possible foul weather. Lancelot's scheme was to enclose all these buildings in a strong wall, and to connect that fort by another wall with the spot at which our skiff was beached.

There was no great difficulty in the construction of such a stockade in itself. Timber enough and to spare was to be had for the chopping, and we had thirty odd pairs of arms and sufficient axes to make that a matter of no difficulty. Nor was there any difficulty as regards the building of such a fort, for Lancelot's knowledge of military matters made him quite capable of planning it out according to the most approved methods of fortification.

We set to work upon the stockade at once, and soon were chopping away for dear life, even Marjorie wielding a light axe, and wielding it well. Many hands, it is said, make light work, and there were enough of us to make the business move pretty quickly. Choosing trees with trunks of a middling thickness, we soon had a great quantity cut down and made of the length that was needed. These we proceeded to set up in the places that Lancelot had marked out, but first we dug deep trenches in the ground so as to ensure their being firmly established, Marjorie taking her share of the spade work with a will. We had not done very much before Abraham Janes, the carpenter, came out of the hut and joined us. He declared that he was now well refreshed, and that he wished to bear his part in the labour; and indeed we were very glad to let him do so, because he was an exceedingly skilful workman, and very ready with the use of saw and hatchet.

CHAPTER XXVI

THE BUSINESS BEGINS

With toil we set up the front of our stockade and a portion of the sides of the parallelogram. It was all loopholed for our musketry, and was firm and strong, being carefully stiffened behind by cross beams and shored up with buttresses of big logs in a manner that, if not thoroughly workmanlike, was at least satisfactory from the point of strength, which was just then our main consideration. Our palisade was about double the height of a man, and in the centres, both front and back, there was a gate, that was held in its place when shut by heavy bars of wood which fitted into holes cut to receive them.

Ere set of sun we had our outworks completed, and found ourselves the possessors of a very creditable stockade, which under ordinary conditions ought, if properly manned and well supplied with ammunition, to resist the attack of a very much greater number than the defending party. It was still in our mind to run out a palisade that should connect our stronghold with the place where the skiff lay, but it was too late, and we were now too exhausted to think of that, for we had worked at our task ever since we had got the alarm, and it was really impossible for us to do more in that work.

But before we rested we conveyed from our boat all our stores and all our arms and ammunition—of which latter, indeed, we had no great quantity, a matter which we had not heeded before, but which now gave us great trouble. We brought in abundance of water, and we had ample provisions, which the island itself had in chief part offered to us, so that we could hold our own very well for a time in case it came to a siege. Our hope, however, was that we might be able to prevent the pirates from effecting a landing at all.

When we went to seek rest for the night we took care to set good guard and to keep strict watch, for a night attack was possible, if it was not very likely.

Though we were all very tired, both bodily and mentally, by reason of the labour of our hands and the strain upon our minds, I do not think that any of us found sleep very easy to come at first. I only know that I lay on my back and stared up at the stars—for the night was too hot to sleep under cover—for long enough. At last I fell asleep, and through sleep into a fitful feverish dream, which chopped and changed from one place and subject to another; but at last it settled down into one decided dream—and that was a good dream, for it was a dream of Marjorie. It seemed that I was walking with her along the downs beyond Sendennis, not far from that place where Lancelot found me blubbering in years gone by, and that I was telling her that I loved her, and that she let me hold her hand while I told her, which showed that she was not averse to my tale, and that when I had done she turned and looked me full in the face, and there was love—love for me—in her eyes.

Then I awoke suddenly and found it was full day, and that Marjorie was bending over me. For the moment I did not recollect where I was, and stared in surprise at the great wooden paling by which we were surrounded. Then recollection of the whole situation came back to me in a flash, and I leapt to my feet.

All around me the men were making preparations for the morning meal, or were engaged in looking to their weapons, testing the sharpness of a cutlass or seeing to the priming of a matchlock. The big door of the stronghold was open, and through it I could see the white beach and the sea-edge, where Lancelot stood scanning the horizon with the spy-glass. The sun was very bright, and I could hear the parrots screaming away in the woods behind us.

'Come outside, Ralph,' said Marjorie. 'I want to speak with you.'

We went out together through the gate into the open, and walked slowly a little way in the direction of the sea. Both of us looked, naturally enough, to that island where our enemies lay. Presently we halted and stood in silence a few minutes, and then Marjorie spoke.

'Ralph,' she said quietly, 'you are my friend, I believe.'

I had it in my heart to cry wild words to her; to tell her again that I loved her then and for ever, but though the words tingled on my lips they never took life and sound. For Marjorie was looking at me so steadfastly and sadly with a strange gravity in the angel-blue of her eyes that I could not speak what she might not wish to hear. So I simply nodded my head and held out my hand and caught hers and clasped it close.

'Ralph,' she said again. 'We fight for the right, but right is not always might, and our enemies may overpower us. If they do—' here I thought she paled a little, but her voice was as firm as ever—'if they do, I want you to promise me one promise.'

I suppose the look in my face assured her that there was nothing she could ask of me that I would not obey, for she went on without waiting for me to speak:

'I have the right to ask you because of some words you once said to me, words which I remember. If the worst comes you must kill me. Hush'—for I gave a groan as she spoke.

'That must be. I have heard enough to know that I must not live if our enemies triumph. If I were alone I should kill myself; if you were not here I should have to ask Lancelot, but you are here and I would rather it happened by your hand.'

It was strange to stand on that quiet shore by that quiet sea and look into that beautiful face and listen to that beautiful voice and hear it utter such words. But my heart thrilled with a wild pride at her prayer.

'I will do your bidding,' I said, and she answered 'I thank you.' We might have been talking of nothing in particular so even were our voices and so simple was our speech. I pressed her hand and let it go. Then, swiftly, she came a little nearer and took my face in her dear hands and kissed me on the forehead, and there are no words in the world sweet enough or sacred enough to interpret my thoughts in that moment. Then she moved away and made to go towards Lancelot, but even as she did so I saw him turn and run towards us along the beach. As soon as he joined us he bade Marjorie go to our hut and blow the horn to bring our people together. After that she was to wait in her own shelter till he came for her. She obeyed him unquestioningly, as she always did in those days of danger, and for a moment Lancelot and I were alone.

'Here they come,' he said very tranquilly. 'See for yourself.' And he handed the spy-glass to me.

As I put it to my eye he added: 'I can't understand where they get their rig from.'

Neither could I. As I looked through the glass I could see that two boats were coming slowly towards us, and that each boat was full of men. It was surprising enough to see them coming in boats, but it was not that which had chiefly surprised either Lancelot or me. Our wonder was caused by the fact that all the men in the boats were clad in scarlet coats, scarlet coats that looked very bright and clean and new.

'Can these be our men at all?' I asked of Lancelot in amazement. I could not for the life of me conceive what other men they could be, but the sight of all those scarlet coats filled me with astonishment.

Lancelot took the spy-glass from me again without replying, and looked long and patiently at the approaching boats.

'Yes,' he said at last, 'they are our men sure enough, for I see the face of Jensen among them. But how on earth has he contrived to deck out all his gang of rascals in the likeness of soldiers?' He paused for a moment; then added thoughtfully: ''Tis our Providence that the Royal Christopher lost her cannon. Yonder stronghold would be no better than so much pasteboard against a couple of the ship's guns.'

We had no time for further converse. The sound of the horn had rallied our party, and soon the whole of our men were gathered about us, staring over the sea at those two moving blots of scarlet. I cast an anxious glance at the face of each man of our little party, and when I had finished I did not feel anxious any more. I could see by the face of every man that he meant to fight and to fight his best.

Lancelot lost no time in getting the men into order and in arranging exactly what was to be done. It was curious, perhaps, although I did not think it curious then, that these men should have accepted so unquestioningly Lancelot's command over them. But they were old soldiers, who had promised to obey Captain Amber, and he had himself devolved his command upon Lancelot. And so, until Lancelot went stark staring mad, which he was not in the least likely to do, they were perfectly prepared to obey him.

I should not be adhering to the spirit of truthfulness which I have observed in setting down these my early experiences if I did not confess that I faced the fact of coming conflict with very mingled emotions. This was the very first time that I had ever seen human beings about to close in bloody strife. Here I found myself standing up with arms in my hands, ready to take away the life of a fellow-creature—to take away the lives of several fellow-creatures, if needs must. Moreover, I knew very well that there were plenty of chances of my getting knocked on the head in this my first scrimmage, and I trembled a little inwardly—though not, as I believe, outwardly—at the thought of my promise to Marjorie. And yet even with that thought a new courage came into my heart. For I immediately resolved that, come what might, I would endeavour to carry myself in such a manner as Marjorie would have me carry myself, namely, as an honest man should, fighting to the best of his ability for what he believed to be the right cause, and not making too much of a fuss about it. And that resolve nerved me better than a dram of spirits would have done, and I set aside the flask from which I had been on the point to help myself.

I do not know if Lancelot felt like that in any degree, and I never presumed to question him on the point afterwards, as there are some topics upon which gentlemen cannot approach each other, however great the degree of intimacy may be between them. But he certainly carried himself as composedly as if we were standing in a ball-room before the dancing began. It is true that he had been brought up to understand the military life and the use of arms, and he had seen a battle fought in the Low Countries, and had fought a duel himself in France with some uncivil fellow. He never looked handsomer, brighter, more gallant than then, and his faded sea-clothes became him as well as the richest gala suit or finest uniform that courtier or soldier ever wore. He had an exquisite neatness of his person ever, and had contrived every day upon that island to shave himself, so that while most of his fellows bore bristling beards, and my own chin was as raspy as a hedgehog, he might have presented himself at the Court of St. James's, so spruce was his appearance.

When all was ready Lancelot drew up his men very soldierly and made them a little speech. He bade them bear in mind that the men who were about to attack us were not merely our own enemies, but the King's; and not merely the King's enemies, but Heaven's, because, being pirates, they sinned against the laws of Heaven as well as the laws of earth. He bade them be sure that they need look for no mercy from such fellows, and that therefore it behoved every man of them to fight his best, both for his own sake and for the sake of his companions; but also he conjured them, if the victory went with them, not to forget that even those pirates were made in God's image, albeit vilely perverted, and that it was our duty as Christians and as soldiers to show them more mercy than they would deal out to us. He ended by reminding them that they were Englishmen, and that a portion of England's honour and glory depended upon the way in which they carried themselves that day. To all of which they listened attentively, every man standing steady as if on parade.

When Lancelot had quite finished he pulled off his hat and swung it in the air, calling upon them to huzza for the King.

Then there went up from our band such a cheer as did my heart good. The island rang for the first time in its life to the huzzaing with which those stout fellows greeted the name of the King. Again and yet again their voices shook the silence with that manly music, and I, while I shouted as loud as the rest of them, glowed with pride to think that courage and loyalty were the same all the world over. Nothing has ever made me prouder than the courage of that knot of men about to engage in a doubtful conflict in a nameless place with a gang of devils, and gallantly cheering for their King before beginning it.

Those men in scarlet must have heard that cheer and been not a little amazed by it. I dare say that by this time Cornelys Jensen had seen us through his spyglass. If so, how he must have cursed at our readiness and at the sight of our stockade!

It was decided by Lancelot that the first thing to do was to prevent the pirates from landing. If they succeeded by untoward chance in effecting a landing, then all of us who were lucky enough to be left alive were to retreat with all speed to the stronghold and fasten ourselves in there. To this end the gate was left open, and in the charge of two men, whose duty it would be to swing it to and bolt it the moment the last of our men had got inside. A few men were left inside the stockade, including the fugitives, to whom we had given arms. The main body of our men were drawn up along the beach, with their muskets ready. Between these and the stockade a few men were thrown out to cover our retreat, if retreat there had to be.

It was anxious work to watch the advance of those two boats with their scarlet crews over that tranquil tropic sea. The water was smooth, as it had been now for days, and their coming was steady and measured. As had been the case ever since we made Fair Island, there was almost no wind, so that their sails were of little service, but their rowing was excellent, as the rowing of good seamen always is. And, villains though they were, those underlings of Jensen's were admirable sailors.

When they were quite near we could recognise the faces of the fellows in the two boats. Cornelys Jensen was in the first boat, and he was dressed out as sumptuously as any general of our army on a field day. For though every man jack of them in the two boats was blazing in scarlet, and though that scarlet cloth was additionally splendid with gold lace, the cloth and the cut of Jensen's coat were finer and better than those of the others, and it was adorned and laced with far greater profusion. With his dark face and evil expression he looked, to my mind, in all his finery more like my lady's monkey in holiday array than man, pirate, or devil, although he was indeed all three.

Every man in those two boats was decked out in scarlet cloth and gold lace— except one. Every man in those two boats was heavily armed with muskets, pistols and cutlasses—except one. The exception was a man who sat by the side of Jensen. He was clad in black, and his face was very pale, and there was an ugly gash of a raw wound across his forehead. I could see that his hands were tied behind him, and in the wantonness of power Jensen had laid his own bare hanger across the prisoner's knees. I knew the captive at once. He was the Reverend Mr. Ebrow, who had so strengthened us by his exhortation during our peril on board the Royal Christopher.

When Lancelot saw whom they had with them and the way that those villains treated their captive I noted that his face paled, and that there came a look into his eyes which I had not often seen there, but which meant no good for Jensen and his scum if Lancelot got the top of them. For Lancelot was a staunch Churchman and a respecter of ministers of God's Word, and as loyal to his religion as he was to his King.

There was one face which I missed out of those boatloads of blackguards, a face which I had very confidently expected to find most prominent amongst them. When I missed it in the first boat I made sure that I should find it in the second, and probably in the place of command; but it was not there either, very much to my surprise. At that crisis in our affairs, at that instant of peril to my life, I was for the moment most perturbed, or at least most puzzled by the fact that I could not find this familiar face among the collection of scarlet-coated scoundrels who were creeping in upon us.

The face that I was looking for was a face that would have gone well enough too with a scarlet coat, for it was a scarlet face in itself. I looked for that red-haired face which I had seen for the first time leering at me over Barbara's shoulders on the last day that ever I set foot within the Skull and Spectacles. I was looking for the face of Jensen's partner in treason—Hatchett.

By this time our enemies had come to within perhaps ten boats' lengths of Fair Island. All this time they had kept silence, and all this while we had kept silence also. But now, as if Lancelot had made up his mind exactly at what point he would take it upon him to act, we assumed the defensive. For Lancelot gave the command to make ready and to present our pieces, and his words came from his lips as clearly and as composedly as if he were only directing some drilling on an English green. In a moment all our muskets were at the shoulder, while Lancelot called out to the pirates that if they rowed another inch nearer he would give the order to fire. Our men were steady men, and, though I am sure that more than one of them was longing to empty his piece into the boats, all remained as motionless as if on parade.

The pirate boats came to a dead stop, and I could see that all the men who were not busy with the oars were gripping their guns. But Jensen kept them down with a gesture. Then, as the boats were steady, he rose to his feet and waved a white handkerchief in sign that he wished for parley. It was part of the foppishness of the fellow that the handkerchief was edged with lace, like a woman's or a grandee's.

Lancelot called out to him to know what he wanted. Jensen shouted back that he wished to parley with us. Lancelot promptly made answer that he needed no parley, that he knew him and his crew for traitors, murderers, and pirates, with whom he would have no dealings save by arms.

At those bold words of his we could see that the fellows in the scarlet coats were furious, and we could guess from their gestures that many of them were urging Jensen to attack us at once, thinking, no doubt, that they might return our fire and, being able to effect a landing before we could reload, might cut us to pieces.

But, whatever their purposes were, Jensen restrained them, and it was a marvel to see the ease with which he ruled those savages. He again addressed himself to Lancelot, warning him that it would be for his peace and the peace of those who were with him to come to some understanding with the invaders. And at last, having spoken some time without shaking Lancelot's resolve,

Jensen asked if he would at least receive an envoy upon the island.

Lancelot was about to refuse again when something crossed his mind, and he shouted back to Jensen to know whom he would send. Jensen, who had probably divined his thoughts, clapped his hand upon the shoulder of that prisoner of his who sat by his side all in black, and called out to Lancelot that he proposed to send the parson as his envoy. To this Lancelot agreed, but I saw that he looked anxious, for it crossed his mind, as he afterwards told me, that this proposition might merely serve as an excuse for the pirate boats to come close, and so give them a better chance of attacking us. However, the pirates made no such attempt. It may be that Jensen, who was quick of wit, guessed Lancelot's thought. The boats remained where they were. We saw the reverend gentleman stand up. One of Jensen's fellows untied his hands, and then without more ado Jensen caught the poor man up by his waistband and straightway flung him into the sea.

A cry of anger broke from Lancelot's lips when he saw this, for he feared that the man might drown. But he was a fair swimmer, and the distance was not so great, so within a few seconds of his plunge he found his depth and came wading towards us with the water up to his middle, looking as wretched as a wet rat, while all the rogues in the boats laughed loud and long at the figure he cut.

"Lancelot Rushed Forward Into the Water."

Lancelot rushed forward into the water to give him his hand, and so drew the poor fellow on to the dry land and amongst us again.

The first thing he did was to assure us—which was indeed hardly necessary, considering his cloth and his character—that he was in no wise leagued with the pirates, but simply and solely a prisoner at their mercy, whose life they had preserved that he might be of use to them as a hostage.

Lancelot called out to the pirate boats to withdraw further back, which they did after he had passed his word that he would confer with them again in a quarter of an hour, after he had heard what their envoy had to say. When they had withdrawn out of gunshot, their scarlet suits glowing like two patches of blood on the water, then Lancelot, still bidding our line to be on guard against any surprise, withdrew with me and the clergyman and two or three of our friends a little way up the beach. And there we called upon Mr. Ebrow to tell us all that he had to tell.

CHAPTER XXVII

AN ILL TALE

It was an ill tale which he had to tell, and he told it awkwardly, for he was not a little confused and put about, both by his wound and by his treatment at the hands of those people. We gave him somewhat to eat and drink, and he munched and sipped between sentences, for he had not fared well with the pirates. We would have given him a change of raiment, too, after his ducking, but this he refused stiffly, saying that he was well enough as he was, and that a wetting would not hurt him. And he was indeed a strong, tough man.

Much of what he had to tell us we knew, of course, already—of the appearance of Jensen on the island, of the attack upon the colonists and the massacre of the most part of them. He himself had got his cut over the head in the fight, a cut that knocked him senseless, so that by the time he came to again the business was over and the pirates were masters of the island.

But he was able to tell us the thing we most wanted to know, the thing which the fugitives could give us no inkling of, and that was how it came to pass that Jensen, whom we all deemed dead and drowned, should have come so calamitously to life again.

It was, it seemed, in this wise. Jensen, who united a madman's cunning to a bad man's daring, saw that my suspicions of him might prove fatal to his plans. Those plans had indeed been, as I had guessed, to seize the Royal Christopher and make a pirate ship of her, with himself for her captain; and to that end he had manned the ship with men upon whom he could rely, many of whom had been pirates before, all of whom were willing to go to any lengths for the sake of plunder and pleasure. But so long as our party were suspicious of him, and had arms in readiness to shoot him and his down at the first show of treachery, it was plain to a simpler man that his precious scheme stood every chance of coming to smoke.

He guessed, therefore, that if we could be led to believe that he was dead and done with our suspicions would be lulled, and he would be left with a fair field to carry out his plan. To that end he devised a scheme to befool us, and, having primed his party as to his purpose, he carried it out with all success.

It was no man's body that went overboard on that night, but merely a mighty beam of wood that one of Jensen's confederates cast over the vessel's side just before he raised the cry of 'Man overboard!' Jensen himself was snugly concealed in the innermost parts of the ship, where he lay close, laughing in his sleeve at us and our credulity. After we left he came out of his hole and made his way to Early Island, as agreed upon with his companions, who, on his arrival, butchered the most of the colonists.

One mystery was disposed of. So was the other mystery—how Jensen and his men came to be so well-armed and so gaily attired. When our expedition was preparing, Captain Marmaduke commissioned Jensen to buy a store of all manner of agricultural and household implements and utensils for the use of the young colony. Now, as such gear was not likely to be of service to Jensen in his piracies, he was at pains to serve his own ends while he pretended to obey the Captain's commands.

He had therefore made up and committed to the hold a quantity of cases which professed to contain what the Captain had commanded. But never a spade or pick, never a roasting-jack or flat-iron, never a string of beads or a mirror for barter with natives was to be found in all those boxes. If our colony had ever by any chance arrived at their goal they would have found themselves in sore straits for the means of tilling the earth and of cooking their food.

The boxes contained instead a great quantity of arms, such as muskets and pistols and cutlasses, together with abundance of ammunition in the shape of powder, bullets and shot. Others of those boxes contained goodlier gear, for Jensen was a vain rogue as well as a clever rogue, and dearly loved brave colours about him and to make a gaudy show. I believe that it was a passion for power and the pomp that accompanies power more than anything else which drove him to be a pirate, and that if he could have been, say, a great Minister of State, who is, after all, often only another kind of pirate, he might have carried himself very well and been looked upon by the world at large as a very decent, public-spirited sort of fellow. I have known men in high office with just such passion for display and dominion as Jensen, and I do not think that there is much to choose between him and them in that regard.

So sundry of those lying boxes were loaded with gay clothing, such as those scarlet coats with which we had now made acquaintance, and which were fashioned on the pattern of those of the bodyguard of His Majesty, only much more flauntingly tricked out with gold lace and gilded buttons. It added a shade of darkness to the treachery of this scoundrel that he should thus presume to parade himself in a parody of such a uniform.

But besides all this there was yet another secret which those same false coffers concealed. He had dealings with shipbuilders at Haarlem, who were noted for their ingenuity and address, and this firm had built for him two large skiffs, which were made in such a fashion that the major part of them could be taken to pieces and the whole packed away in a small space with safety and convenience for his purpose. These vessels were as easily put together as taken to pieces, and were as serviceable a kind of boat as ever vessel carried. And so there was the rascal well prepared to make sure of our ship.

It makes my heart bleed now, after all these years, to think how the fellow deceived my dear patron, and how the Royal Christopher went sailing the seas with that secret in her womb, and that we all walked those decks night after night and day after day, and never suspected the treason that lay beneath our feet.

But we never did suspect it, and when the time came for us to leave the ship in a hurry we had little thought in our minds of taking agricultural implements or household gear or articles of barter with us. So they lay there snugly in the hold, and Jensen with them, and Jensen was busy and happy in his wicked way in getting at them, and in laughing as he did so over our folly in being deceived by him.

It seems that after the departure of Lancelot and our little party certain of the sailors, as agreed upon beforehand, made their way back to the ship, and in the dead of night transported the greater quantity of the weapons and ammunition. They put the skiffs together, too, and lowered them over the side. The camp had gone to rest when Jensen, shrieking like a fiend, leaped from his concealment among the trees and gave the signal for attack. The butchery was brief. The few men who were armed found that their weapons had been rendered useless, but even if their murderers had not taken that precaution their victims could have made no sort of a stand. They were taken by surprise. The horrible cries that the pirates made as they rushed from their ambush helped to dishearten the colonists, for they took those noises for the war-cries of savages, and they yielded to the panic. A very few escaped from the slaughter, and hid themselves in the woods in the centre of the island. The manner of their escape I have already related. It seemed from what the parson now told us that Jensen made little effort to pursue them, feeling confident that they must perish miserably from hunger and thirst, if not from wild beasts, in the jungle.

The first use Jensen made of his triumph was to bring over to the island from the wreck everything that he believed to be needful for the comfort and adornment of his person and the persons of his following. All the arms and ammunition that his malign thoughtfulness had provided, all the fine clothes that he had hidden away, all the store of wines and strong waters that still remained upon the ship were carefully disembarked and brought to Early Island. He dressed himself and his followers up in the smart clothes that we had seen, called himself king of the island, made his companions take a solemn oath of allegiance to him and sign it with their blood, and then they all gave themselves up to an orgie.

For, bad as all this was to tell and to listen to, there was still worse to be told and heard. To treachery and bloodshed were added treachery and lust. The cup of Jensen's iniquity was more than full. It ran over and was spilt upon the ground, crying out to Heaven for vengeance.

There were, as you know, women among our colonists—not many, but still some, the wives of some of the settlers, the daughters and sisters of others. None of these were hurt when Jensen and his fellow-fiends made their attack —none of them, unhappily for themselves, were killed. My cheeks blazed with shame and wrath as I listened to what the parson had to say, and if Jensen had been before me I would have been rejoiced to pistol him with my own hand.

The women were parcelled out among the men as the best part of their booty. There was not a wickeder place on God's earth at that hour than the island, and its sins, as I thought, should be blotted out by a thunderbolt from Heaven.

Yet there is something still worse to come, as I take it. In all this infamy Jensen reserved for himself the privilege of a deeper degree of infamy. For he told Hatchett, it seems, that he must give up Barbara, and when Hatchett laughed in his face Jensen shot him dead where he stood and took her by force. Such was the terror the man inspired that no one of all his fellows presumed to avenge Hatchett, or even to protest against the manner of his death. As for the woman, as for Barbara, she was a strong woman, and she loved Hatchett with all her heart, and she fought, I believe, hard. But if she was strong, Jensen was stronger, and merciless. He had everything his own way at the island; he had his arts of taming people, and the parson told me that he had tamed Barbara.

I have had to set these wrongs down here for the sake of truth, and to justify our final deeds against Jensen and his gang. I have set them down as barely and as briefly as possible, for there are some things so terrible that they scarcely bear the telling. I cannot be more particular; the whole bad business was hideous in the extreme, with all the hideousness that could come from a mind like Jensen's—a mind begotten of the Bottomless Pit.

But in all my sorrow I was grateful to Heaven that Marjorie had not been left upon that other island. Better for her to die here by the hand of the man who loved her than to have been on that island at the mercy of such men. Thank God, thank God, thank God! I said to myself again and again. I could say nothing more, I could think nothing more, only thank God, thank God!

CHAPTER XXVIII

WE DEFY JENSEN

That unhappy Barbara! Her sin had found her out indeed. She was a wicked woman, for she had been part and parcel in the treason, she had been hand and glove with the traitors. But she did not mean such wickedness to the women-folk, and she did what she had done for her husband's sake, thinking that he would be a pirate king and she his consort. This was what she meant when she had called herself a queen. With such falsehoods had Jensen stuffed the ears of the man and his wife, snaring them to their fate. As I had loved her once, so I pitied her now. She had shared in a great crime, but it would be hard to shape a greater penalty for her sin.

By the time that the parson had finished his story we who were listening to him felt dismal, and we looked at each other grimly.

'What is the first thing to be done?' Lancelot said softly, more to himself than as really asking any advice upon the matter from us.

'Fire a volley upon those devils when they draw near, and so rid the earth of them,' I suggested.

Lancelot shook his head.

'They are under the protection of a flag of truce——' he began, when I interrupted him hotly.

'What right,' I raged at him, 'what right have such devils to the consideration of honourable warfare and of honourable men?'

Lancelot sighed.

'None whatever; but that does not change us from being honourable men and from carrying on our contest according to the rules of honourable warfare. They are devils, ruffians, what you will, but we—we are gentlemen, and we have passed our word. We cannot go back from that.'

I know very well that I blushed a fiery red, from rage against our enemy and shame at Lancelot's reproof. But I said nothing, and Mr. Ebrow spoke.

'Mr. Amber,' he said, clasping Lancelot's hand as he spoke, 'you are in the right, in the very right, as a Christian soldier and a Christian gentleman. Their hour will come without our anticipating it.' And then he wrung my hand warmly, in token that he understood my feelings too, and did not overmuch blame me.

'One thing at least is certain,' said Lancelot. 'You must not return to the mercies of those villains.'

Mr. Ebrow drew himself stiffly up. He was wet and weary, and the ugly cut on his forehead did not add to the charm of his rugged face, but just at that moment he seemed handsome.

'Mr. Amber,' he said, 'I passed my word to those men that I would return after I had given you their message, and I will keep my word.'

'But,' said Lancelot, 'they will kill you!'

'It is possible,' said the man of God calmly. 'It is very probable. But I have in my mind the conduct of the Roman Regulus. Should I, who am a minister of Christ, be less nice in my honour than a Pagan?'

'Nay, but if we were to restrain you by force?' asked Lancelot.

'Mr. Amber,' Ebrow answered, 'it was your duty just now to administer a reproof to your friend; I hope you will not force me to reprove you in your turn. I have given my word, and there is an end of it; and if you were to hold me by the strong hand I should think you more worthy to consort with those pirates than with me.'

It was now Lancelot's turn to blush. Then he gripped Mr. Ebrow's hand.

'I beg your pardon,' he said, and there were tears in his eyes as he spoke. 'You have taught me a noble lesson.'

Mr. Ebrow seemed as if he would be going, but I stayed him.

'Reverend sir,' said I, 'may I make so bold as to ask what is this message that you have to deliver to us?'

For, as a matter of fact, we had so plied him with questions, and he had been so busy in answering us, that he had not as yet delivered to us the pirates' message, of which he was the spokesman.

There came a spot of colour on his grey jaws as I spoke.

'True. I fear I make but a poor intermediary,' he said. 'The pirates propose, in the first place, that you make common cause with them, and recognise the authority of Cornelys Jensen as your captain, in the which case Cornelys Jensen guarantees you your share of the spoiling of the Royal Christopher, and in future a fitting proportion of whatever profits may come from their enterprises.'

'I suppose you do not expect us to consider that proposition?' said Lancelot.

Mr. Ebrow almost smiled.

'No, indeed,' he said, 'and I do but discharge my promise in repeating it to you. I must tell you too that he added that he was wishful to make your sister his wife.'

There came into Lancelot's eyes the ugliest look I ever saw there, and for myself I know not how I looked, I know only how I felt, and I will not put my feelings into words. I suppose Mr. Ebrow understood us and our silence, for he went on with his embassy. 'In the second place, then, they call upon you to swear that you will take no part against them, and will, on the contrary, do your endeavour to protect them in case they should be attacked by other forces.'

'That also needs no consideration,' said Lancelot.

Mr. Ebrow nodded.

'Of course not, of course not. Then, in the third place, they call upon you to throw down your weapons and to surrender yourselves to them as prisoners of war, in which case they pledge themselves to respect your lives and preserve you all as hostages for their own safety.'

'And if we refuse even this offer,' Lancelot asked, 'what is to happen then?'

'In that case,' said Mr. Ebrow, 'they declare war against you; they will give you no quarter——'

'Let them wait till they are asked!' I broke in; but Lancelot rested his hand restrainingly upon my arm.

'As for the matter of quarter,' he said, 'it may prove in the end more our business to give it than to seek for it. Quarter we may indeed give in this sense, that even those villains shall not be killed in cold blood if they are willing to surrender. But every man that we take prisoner shall most assuredly be tried for his life for piracy and murder upon the high seas. Will you be so good as to tell those men from me that if they at once surrender the person of Cornelys Jensen and their own weapons they shall be treated humanely, kept in decent confinement, and shall have the benefit of their conduct when the time for trial comes? But this offer will not hold good after to-day, and if they attempt again to approach the island they shall be fired upon.'

'Well and good, sir,' said Mr. Ebrow. 'Have you anything more to say, for my masters did but give me a quarter of an hour, and I feel sure that my time must be expired by now?'

'Only this,' answered Lancelot, 'that if they want to fly their black flag over this island they must come and take it from us.'

I never saw Lancelot look more gallant, with courage and hope in his mien, and the soft wind fretting his hair. But the brightness faded away from his face a moment after as he added:

'It grieves me to heart, sir, that you have to return to those ruffians.'

Mr. Ebrow extended his hand to Lancelot with a wintry smile.

'It is my duty. I do but follow my Master's orders, to do all in His Name and for His glory.'

He wrung Lancelot's hand and mine, and the hand of every man in our troop. He gave us his blessing, and then, turning, walked with erect head to the sea.

As soon as the pirates saw him coming they rowed their boat a little nearer in, when they rested on their oars, while we stood to our guns and the parson waded steadily out into the deeper water.

When he reached their boat they dragged him on board roughly, and we could see from their gestures and his that he was telling them the result of the interview with us.

The telling did not seem to give any great satisfaction to the villains, and least of all to Jensen, for he struck the parson a heavy blow in the face with his clenched hand that felled him, tumbling down among the rowers. Then Jensen turned and shook his fist in our direction, and shouted out something that we could not hear because of the distance and the slight wind.

It seemed to me as if for a moment Jensen had a mind to order his boats to advance and try to effect a landing, and I wished this in my heart, for I was eager to come to blows with the villains, and confident that we should prove a match for them.

But it would seem as if discretion were to prevail with them, in which, indeed, they were wise, for to attempt to land even a more numerous force in the face of our well-armed men would have been rash and a rough business. We saw the boats sweep round and row rapidly away, and we watched those scarlet coats dwindle into red spots in the distance.

126

CHAPTER XXIX

THE ATTACK AT LAST

In what I am going to tell there will be little of Marjorie for a while, for sorely against her will we refused to rank her as a fighting man and made her keep within shelter, though busy in many ways making ready for the inevitable attack.

Nothing happened on the next day or the next to disturb our quiet and the beauty of the weather. For all that was evident to the contrary we might very well have been the sole inhabitants of that archipelago, the sole children of those seas, with Marjorie for our queen.

We did not hope, however, nor indeed did we wish, that we had heard the last of our enemies. There was a moment even when Lancelot considered the feasibility of our making an attack upon Early Island in the hope of rescuing some of the captives. But the plan was only suggested to be dismissed. For every argument which told against their attempting to make an attack upon us told with ten times greater force against our making an attack upon them. They outnumbered us; they were perhaps better armed. The odds were too heavily against us. But our hearts burnt within us at the thought of the captives.

We had evidently come in for one of those spells of fine weather which in those regions so often follow upon such a storm as had proved the undoing of the Royal Christopher. If the conditions had been different our lives would have been sufficiently enviable. Fair Island deserves its name; we had summer, food and water; so far as material comfort went, all was well with us.

But mere material comfort could not cheer us much. We were in peril ourselves; we were yet more concerned for the peril of Captain Amber, of whose fortunes and whose whereabouts we knew absolutely nothing. If he failed to meet a ship he was to return to Early Island. What might not be his fate? To diminish in some degree the chance of this catastrophe, we resolved to erect some signal on the highest point of Fair Island, in the hope that it would have the result of attracting his attention and leading him to suppose that the whole of the ship's company were settled down there.

There was no difficulty in the making of such a signal. We had a flag with us in the boat, and all that it was necessary to do was to fix it to the summit of one of the tall trees that crowned the hill which sprang from the centre of Fair

Island. In a few hours the flag was flying gallantly enough from its primitive flag-staff, a sufficiently conspicuous object even with a gentle breeze to serve, as we hoped, our turn.

In the two days that followed upon the visit of the pirates we were busy victualling the stockade and supplying it with water, looking to our arms and ammunition, and, which was of first importance, in building a strong fence, loopholed like the stockade. This fence or wall led down to where our boat lay, and enabled us to protect it from any attempt of the pirates to carry it off or to destroy it. In work of this kind the eight-and-forty hours passed away as swiftly as if they had been but so many minutes.

On the afternoon of the third day all our preparations were completed, and I was convinced that within that stockade our scanty force could keep the pirates at bay for a month of Sundays, so long as they did not succeed in getting sufficiently close to employ fire as a means of forcing an entrance. But though I felt cheered I noticed that there was no corresponding cheerfulness in Lancelot's face. He never looked despondent, but he looked dissatisfied.

I drew him aside and asked what troubled him.

'The moon troubles me,' he answered.

'The moon!' I said in astonishment.

'Yes,' he answered, 'the moon—or rather, the absence of the moon. Last night was the moon's last night, and to-night we shall be in darkness after sunset. It is under cover of that darkness that, some time or another, to-night or another night, sooner or later, the pirates will make an attempt to land. For you may be sure that they have not forgotten us, and that they would be glad enough to pull down yonder flag.'

I felt in my heart that what Lancelot said was true enough, but I tried to put a bold face upon it.

'After all,' I said, 'the darkness will be as bad for them as it is for us.'

'No,' Lancelot said; 'they can steer well enough by the stars. If I thought that they could get round to the back of the island and fall upon us that way, I should feel that we were in a very bad case indeed. But of that I have no fear. There is no place for landing in that part, and if there were they would find it hard enough to force their way through the woods. No, no; they will come as they came before.'

I asked him what he thought was the best thing to do. He replied that the only thing was to keep a very sharp look-out, and to fight hard if it came to fighting, a pithy sentence, which seemed to me to sum up the whole art of war

—at least, so far as we were concerned who dwelt on Fair Island. To make assurance doubly sure, however, Lancelot did during the day place a man by the flag-staff, from which point, as the hill ran up into a high peak, he would be able to sweep the sea in all directions. With regard to the night, Lancelot showed me how fortunate it was that he had brought the fireworks with us, as, at a pinch, in the darkness, we could get a gleam of light for a minute by firing them.

I was getting so unstrung by all these alarms and watchings that I began to wish that the pirates would come once for all that we might have done with them. For I had confidence in our side and the certainty of its winning which was scarcely logical, maybe, but which, after all, I think is a great deal better than feeling suspicious of the strength of one's own side or speculative as to the merits of one's own cause.

How often afterward, in other places and amid perils as great, or indeed ten times greater, have I remembered that night with all its agony of expectation!

The main part of our little garrison was ensconced in the stockade and sleeping, or seeking to sleep, for every man of us knew well enough that he needed to have all his energies when the struggle came, and that the more rest he got beforehand the better the fighting trim he would be in afterward.

We had sentinels posted at different points along that portion of the coast where landing was possible, and though we had been grateful to it before for being such an easy place to land upon, we could almost have wished in our hearts now that it had been less easy of access.

In front of the stockade, but some considerable distance from it, and on the sloping land that was nigh to the beach, we had thrown up a kind of intrenchment, behind which we could kneel and fire, and under whose cover we hoped to be able to make a good account of assailants. I was on guard here at night, and I paced up and down in front of it thinking of all the chances that had happened since I sailed in the Royal Christopher; and I pleased myself by recalling every word that Marjorie had said to me, or in thinking of all the words that I should like to say to her.

Suddenly my thoughts were brought from heaven to earth by a sound as of a splash in the water. It might have been but a sweep of a sea-bird's wing as it stooped and wheeled in its flight over the sea, but it set my pulses tingling and all my senses straining to hear more and to see something.

The sea that lay so little away from me was all swallowed up in darkness. I could see nothing to cause me alarm. The quiet of the night seemed to breathe a deep peace that invited only to thoughts of sleep. But I was as wide awake as a startled hare, and I listened with all my ears and peered into the blackness. Was it my heated fancy, I asked myself, or did I indeed hear faint sounds coming to me from where the sea lay?

I whistled softly a note something like our English starling's—a signal that had been agreed upon between Lancelot and me. In a very few seconds he was at my side.

As I told him of my suspicions Lancelot peered into the darkness, listening very carefully, and now both he and I felt certain that we could hear sounds, indistinct but regular, coming from the sea.

'They are doing what I thought they would,' Lancelot whispered to me. Lancelot's voice had this rare quality, that when he whispered every syllable was as clear as if he were crying from the housetops. 'They have chosen this dark night to attack us, and they are rowing with muffled oars. We must do our best to give them a wild welcome. It is well we have those fireworks; they will serve our turn now.'

He slipped away from my side and was swallowed up in the darkness. But he soon came back to my side.

'All is ready,' he said.

He had been from man to man, and now every one was at his post. The bulk of our little body crouched down behind the breastwork while four men were stationed by the open gates of the stockade to allow us to make our retreat there. Those who were behind the breastwork knew that when Lancelot gave the word they were to fire in the direction of the sea. Lancelot had his lights ready, and we waited anxiously for the flare.

The seconds seemed to lengthen out into centuries as we lay there, listening to those sounds growing louder, though even at their loudest they might very well have escaped notice if one were not watching for them. At last they came to an end altogether, and we could just catch a sound as of a succession of soft splashes in the water.

Lancelot whispered close to my ear: 'They are getting out in the shallow water to draw their boats in. We shall have a look at them in an instant.'

While I held my breath I was conscious that Lancelot was busy with his flint and steel. His was a sure hand and a firm stroke. I could hear the click as he struck stone and metal together; there was a gleam of fire as the fuse caught, and then in another instant one of his fireworks rose in a blaze of brightness. It only lasted for the space of a couple of seconds, but in that space of time it showed us all that we had to see and much more than we wished to see.

As our meteor soared in the air the space in front of us was lit with a light as clear as the light of dawn, though in colour it was more like that of the moon —at least, as I have seen her rays represented often enough since in stage plays. Before us the sea rippled gently against the sand, and in the shallows we saw the pirates as clearly as we had seen them on the day when they first came to the island.

There were now three boatloads of them, and the boats were more fully manned than before. Many of the men were still in the boats, but the greater part were in the water, barelegged, and were stealthily urging the boats ashore. They were doing the work quietly, and made little noise. It was the strangest sight I had ever seen, this sight of those men in their scarlet coats, that looked so glaring in that blue light, with their gleaming weapons, all moving towards us with murder in their minds.

In their amazement at the flame the pirates paused for an instant, and in that instant Lancelot gave the order we itched for.

'Fire!'

Then the silence was shattered by the discharge of our pieces in a steady volley. All the island rang with the report, and at that very instant the rocket on its home curve faded and went out with a kind of wink, and darkness swallowed us all up again.

But what darkness! The darkness had been still; now it was full of noises. The echo of the report of our volley rang about us; from the woods came clamour, the screaming and chattering of wakened birds, and we could even hear the brushing of their wings as they flew from tree to tree in their terror. But in front of us the sounds were the most terrible of all; the splashing of bodies falling into the water, the shrieks of wounded men, the howls and curses of the astonished and infuriated enemy. We could not tell what hurt we had done, but it must have been grave, for we had fired at close range, and we were all good marksmen.

But we could not hope that we had crippled our invaders, or done much toward equalising our forces. For, as it had seemed in that moment of illumination, we were outnumbered by well-nigh two to one.

There was no need to fire another light; it was impossible that we could hope to hold our own in the open, and our enemies would be upon us before we had time to reload, so there was nothing for it but to retreat to the stockade with all speed.

Lancelot gave the order, and in another instant we were racing for the stockade, bending low as we ran, for the pirates had begun to fire in our direction. But their firing was wild, and it hit none of us; and it stopped as suddenly as it began, for they soon perceived that it was idle waste of powder and ball in shooting into the darkness.

Luckily for us, we knew every inch of our territory by heart, and could make our way well enough to the stockade in the gloom, while we could hear the pirates behind splashing and stumbling as they landed.

But as they were taken aback by the suddenness of our assault and its result, they were not eager to advance into the night, and, as I guessed, waited awhile after landing from their boats.

As for us, we did not pause until we had passed, every one of us, between the gates of our stockade, and heard them close behind us, and the bar fall into its place. The first thing I saw in the dim light was the face of Marjorie, fair in its pale patience. She had a pistol in her hand, and I knew why she held it.

CHAPTER XXX

OUR FLAG COMES DOWN

We lay still inside our fortalice for awhile, listening, as well as the throbbing of our pulses would allow, to try and hear what our invaders were doing.

We could hear the sound of their voices down on the beach, and the splashing they made in the water as they dragged their dead or wounded comrades out of the water and hauled their boats close up to the shore. But beyond this we heard nothing, though the air was so still, now that the screaming of the birds had died away, that we felt sure that we must hear the sound of any advance in force.

Lancelot whispered to me that it was possible that they might put off their assault until daybreak. They were in this predicament, that if they lit any of the lights which we made no doubt they carried, in order to ascertain the plight that they were in, they would make themselves the targets for our muskets. But the one thing certain was that, under the control of a man like Jensen, they would most certainly not rest till they tried to get the better of us.

That Jensen himself was not among the disabled we felt confident, for Lancelot, who had a fine ear, averred that he could distinguish the sound of Jensen's voice down on the beach, which afterward proved to be so, for Jensen, unable to distinguish in the darkness the amount of injury that his army had sustained, was calling over from memory the name of each man of his gang. Every pirate who answered to his name stated the nature of his wounds, if he had any. Those who made no answer Jensen counted for lost, and of these latter there were no less than three.

There was something terrible in the sense of a darkness that was swarming with enemies. We were not wholly in obscurity inside our enclosure, for we had a couple of the boat's lanterns, which shed enough light to enable us to see each other, and to look to our weapons, without allowing any appreciable light to escape between the timbers of our fortification. Soon all our muskets were loaded again. Lancelot appointed one of the men who came to us on the raft, and who was still too weak for active service, as a loader of guns, that in case of attack we could keep up a steady firing. Happily for us, our supply of ammunition was tolerably large.

For some time, however, we were left in peace. The blackness upon which the pirates had counted as an advantage had proved their bane. So there was nothing for them to do but to wait with what patience they could for the dawn.

The dawn did come at last, and I never watched its coming with more anxiety. Often and often in those days when I believed myself to be fathom-deep in love I used to lie awake on my bed and watch the dawn filling the sky, and find in its sadness a kind of solace for mine own. For a sick spirit there is always something sad about the breaking of the day. Perhaps, if I had been like those who know the knack of verses, I should have worked off my ill-humours in rhyme, and slept better in consequence, and greeted the dawn with joy. Wonder rather than joy was in my mind on this morning as the sky took colour and the woods stirred with the chatter of the birds. For the pirates had disappeared! Their boats lay against the beach, but there was, as it seemed to us at first, no visible sign of their masters.

We soon discovered their whereabouts, however. They had groped, under cover of night, to the woods, and we soon had tokens of their presence. For by-and-by we could hear them moving in the wood, and could catch the gleam of their scarlet coats and the shine upon their weapons.

In the wood they were certainly safe from us, if also we were, though in less measure, safe from them. As I have said, the wooded hill ran at a sharp incline at some distance from the place where we had set up our stockade, so we were not commanded from above, and, no matter how high the pirates climbed, they could not do us a mischief in that way by firing down on to us.

They did climb high, but with another purpose, for presently we saw, with rage in our eyes and hearts, one bit of business they were bent on. Our flag fluttered down like a wounded bird, and it made me mad to think that it was being hauled down by those rascals, and that we had no art to prevent them.

Could we do nothing? I asked Lancelot impatiently. Could we not make a sortie and destroy the boats that lay down there all undefended? But Lancelot shook his head. The way to the sea was doubtless covered by our enemies in the wood. We should only volunteer for targets if we attempted to stir outside our stockade. There was nothing for it but to wait.

I think that it must have enraged the pirates to find us so well protected that there was no means of taking us unawares or of creeping in upon us from the rear. With the daylight they essayed to hurt us by firing from the hill; but from the lie of the ground their shots did us no harm, either passing over our heads or striking the wall of our stronghold and knocking off a shower of splinters, but doing no further damage. We, on the contrary, were able to retaliate, firing through our loopholes up the slope at the red jackets in the woods, and with this much effect, that soon the scarlet rascals ceased to show themselves, and kept well under cover. We felt very snug where we were, and fit to stand a siege for just so long as our victuals and water held out. Then, if the pirates remained upon the island, famine would compel us to a sortie in the hope of clearing them from the woods, an adventure in which our chances of success seemed to kick the balance.

But it did not come to that. About an hour before noon those of us who were at the loopholes saw the shine of a scarlet coat among the trees on the nearest slope, but before there was time to aim a musket something white fluttered above it. It was, as it proved, but a handkerchief tied to a ramrod, but it was a flag of truce for all that, and a flag of truce is respected by gentlemen of honour, whoever carries it.

When the white flag had fluttered long enough for him who held it to make sure that it must have been seen by us, the bearer came out from the cover of the wood and walked boldly down the slope. For all the distance the sharp-sighted among us knew him at once for Cornelys Jensen, and it came into my mind that perhaps Lancelot might refuse to accept him as an emissary. Lancelot, however, said nothing, but stood quietly waiting while the man came nearer. But when he came within pitch of voice Lancelot called out to him to come to a halt.

Jensen stopped at once and waited till Lancelot again called out to him to ask what he wanted. Jensen replied that he came under the protection of a flag of truce; that he wished to come to terms with Captain Amber—for so he called him—if it were by any means possible; that he was alone and unarmed, and trusted himself to our honour. Thereupon Lancelot called back to him to come nearer, and he would hear what he had to say. We had driven some great nails that we had with us into one of the posts of our wall to serve as a kind of ladder, and by these nails Lancelot lifted himself to the top of the palisade, and sat there waiting for Jensen's approach. I begged him not to expose himself, but he answered that there was no danger, so long as Jensen remained within short range of half a dozen of our guns, that the fellows in the woods would make himself a target. And so he sat there as coolly as if he were in an ingle, whistling 'Tyburn Tree' softly to himself as Jensen drew near.

CHAPTER XXXI

A PIECE OF DIPLOMACY

When Jensen was within a few feet of the stockade he halted, and saluted Lancelot with a formal gravity that seemed grotesque under the circumstances. I will do the rascal this justice, that he looked well enough in his splendid coat, though his carriage was too fantastical—more of the stage player than the soldier. Lancelot, looking down at the fellow without returning his salutation, asked him what he wanted.

'Come, Captain Amber,' said Jensen boldly, 'you know what I want very well. I want to come to terms. Surely two men of the world like us ought to be able to make terms, Captain Amber.'

'I do not carry the title of Captain,' Lancelot answered, 'and I have no more in common with you than mere life. My only terms are the unconditional surrender of yourself and your accomplices. In their case some allowance may be made. In yours—none!'

Jensen shrugged his shoulders and smiled with affability at Lancelot's menaces.

'The young cock cackles louder than the old cock ever crowed,' he said; but he said it more good-humouredly than sneeringly, and it was evident that he was more than willing to propitiate Lancelot. 'We ought to make terms, for we are both at a loose end here, and might at least agree not to annoy each other. For you see, Lieutenant—if you will take that title—that as you judge you shall be judged. If you have no terms for us we will have no terms for you.'

It was a proof of his own vanity that he thus thrust a title upon Lancelot, thinking to please him, for when Lancelot, calling him by his surname, told him again that he had no terms to make with him, he drew himself up with an offended air and said:

'I call myself Captain Jensen, if you please.'

'It does not please me,' Lancelot retorted, 'to call you anything but a pirate and a rogue. Go back to your brother rogues at once!'

To my surprise, Jensen kept his temper, and seemed only hurt instead of angry at Lancelot's attack.

'Hot words,' he said quietly, 'hot words. Upon my honour, you do me wrong,

Lieutenant Amber, for I persist in respecting the courtesies of war. I wish with all my heart that we could agree, but if we cannot we cannot, and there's an end of it. But there is another matter I wish to speak about.' He paused, as if waiting for permission, and when Lancelot bade him be brief, he went on: 'We have one among us who is more inclined to your party than to mine. I mean your reverend friend Parson Ebrow.'

For my part I was glad to hear that the poor man was still alive, for I feared that the pirates had killed him after their first attempt. But I saw Lancelot's face flush with anger, and his voice shook as he called out that if any harm came to Mr. Ebrow he would hold every man of the gang responsible for his life.

'Harm has come to him already,' Jensen answered; 'but not from us, but from you, his friends. He was hurt in the boats last night by your fire.'

At this Lancelot gave a groan, and we all felt sick and sorry, while Jensen, who knew that we could hear, though he could only see Lancelot, smiled compassionately.

'Do not be alarmed,' he said. 'The godly man is not mortally wounded. Only his face, which was always far from comely, has not been bettered by a shot that travelled across the side of the left cheek from jaw to ear. Now, another man in my place, Lieutenant, knowing the store you set by the parson, might very well use him to drive a bargain with you. He is no friend of ours, and the use upon him of a little torture might induce you to think better of the terms you deny.'

Lancelot grew pale, and he made as if he would speak, but Jensen delayed him with a wave of the arm.

'Pray let me conclude, Lieutenant Amber,' he went on. 'Another man, having such a hostage, might use him pretty roughly. But I am not of that kidney. I want to fight fair. The reverend gentleman is no use to me. We want no chaplain. He is a friend of yours, and if we win the day some of you will be glad of his ghostly offices. But he is in our way, and I cannot answer for the temper of my people if he exhorts us any more. So I shall be heartily obliged if you will take him off our hands and relieve me of the responsibility of his presence.'

I had listened to this, as you may believe, in some amazement, and Lancelot seemed no less surprised. 'What do you mean?' he asked; and Jensen answered him:

'I mean what I say. You can have your parson. Two of my men, with this flag, will bring him down, for the poor gentleman is too feeble to walk alone from loss of blood, and leave him in your charge. After that we will send no more messages, but fight it out as well as we can till one or other wins the day.'

He took off his hat as he spoke and made Lancelot a bow; and this time Lancelot returned his salutation.

'I can only thank you for your offer,' Lancelot said, 'and accept it gladly. If I cannot change my terms, at least be assured that this charity shall be remembered to your credit.'

'I ask no more,' Jensen replied; 'and you shall have your man within the half-hour.'

With that he clapped his hat proudly upon his head again, and turning on his heel marched away in a swaggering fashion, while Lancelot slipped down again into the shelter of the house. In a few minutes Jensen's red coat had disappeared among the trees, and then we all turned and stared at each other.

'The devil is not so black as he is painted, after all,' Lancelot said to me, 'if there is a leaven of good in Cornelys Jensen. But I shall be heartily glad to have Mr. Ebrow among us, for if the worst come it will be better to perish with us than to lie at their mercy.'

I did not altogether relish Lancelot's talk about our perishing, for I had got it into my head that we were more than a match for the pirates, with all their threats and all their truculence, and my friend's readiness to face the possibility of being victims instead of victors dashed my spirits. But I thought of Marjorie, and felt that we must win or—and then my thoughts grew faint and failed me, but not my promise and my resolve.

We had not waited very long after Jensen's departure when we saw signs of the fulfilment of his promise. Three men came out of the wood where he had entered, two in scarlet and one in black. We could see that the two men in scarlet were supporting the man in black, who seemed to be almost unable to move, and as the three drew nearer we could see, at first with a spy-glass and soon without, that he in the middle had his face all bound about with bloody cloths. At this sight all our hearts grew hot with anger and pity, and there was not one of us that did not long to be the first to reach out a helping hand to the parson. We could see, as the group came nearer, that Jensen's men were not handling their captive very tenderly. Though his limbs seemed so weak that his feet trailed on the ground, they made shift to drag him along at a walk that was almost a trot, as if their only thought was to be rid as soon as possible of their burden, whose moanings we could now plainly hear as he was jerked forward by his escort. It seemed such a shocking thing that a man so good and of so good a calling should be thus maltreated that, to speak for myself, it called for all my sense of the obligations of a white flag to stay me from sending a bullet in the direction of his cowardly companions. I could see that Lancelot was as much angered as I, by the pallor of his face and the way in which he clenched his hands.

However, in a few seconds more the pirates had hauled their helpless prisoner to within a few feet of our fortress. Then, to the increase of our indignation, they flung him forward with brutal oaths, so that he fell grovelling on his injured face just in front of our doorway, and while he lay prone one of the ruffians dealt him a kick which made him groan like a dog. After they had done this the two red-jackets drew back a few paces and waited, according to the agreement, laughing the while at the plight of the clergyman.

In a moment, obedient to a word from Lancelot, a dozen hands lifted the beam and swung the door back. Lancelot sprang forward, followed hard by me, to succour our unhappy friend; and between us we lifted him from the ground, though with some effort, for he seemed quite helpless and senseless with his ill-treatment and the fall, and unable to give us the least aid in supporting him. Jensen's two brutes jeered at us for our pains, bidding us mind our sermon-grinder and the like, with many expletives that I shall not set down. Indeed, their speech and behaviour so discredited their mission that it would have jeopardised their safety, for all their flag of truce, with a commander of less punctiliousness than Lancelot. But he, without paying heed to their mutterings, propped the prisoner up stoutly, and carried him, huddled and trailing, toward the stockade. As we moved him he moaned feebly, and kept up this moaning as we carried him inside the stockade and drew him toward the most sheltered corner to lay him down.

My heart bled for the parson in his weakness, with his head all swathed in bloody bandages, and I shuddered to think what his face would be like when we took off those coverings. I turned to pile some coats together for him to rest upon, but I was still looking at him as he hung helpless against Lancelot, when, in a breath, before my astounded eyes, the limp form stiffened, and Mr. Ebrow, stiff and strong, flung himself upon Marjorie and caught her in his arms. Quickly though the act was done, I still had time to think that Mr. Ebrow's calamities had turned his brain, and to feel vexation at the increase to our difficulties with a mad-man in our midst. In the next instant I saw that Mr. Ebrow was squatting on the ground behind Marjorie, sheltered by her body, which he held pinioned to his with his left arm, while his right hand held a pistol close to her forehead. Then a voice that was not the voice of Mr. Ebrow called out that Marjorie was his prisoner, and that if any man moved to rescue her he would blow the girl's brains out. And the voice that made these threats was the voice of Cornelys Jensen!

I cannot tell you how astounded we were at this sudden turn in our fortunes.

Our garrison, taken by surprise, had left their posts every man, and stood together at one end of our parallelogram. Lancelot stood still and white as a statue. I leant against the wall and gasped for breath like a man struck silly. Marjorie lay perfectly still in the grasp of her enemy, and Jensen's eyes between the bandages seemed to survey the whole scene with a savage sense of mastery. He was so well protected where he crouched by Marjorie's body that no one dared to fire, or, indeed, for the moment, to do anything but stare in stupefaction. The stroke was so sudden, the change so unexpected, the dash so bold, that we were at a disadvantage, and for a space no one moved.

In a loud voice Jensen called upon every man to throw down his weapons, swearing furiously that if they did not do so he would kill Marjorie. Marjorie, on her part, though she could not free herself from Jensen's hold—for Jensen had the clasp and the hold of a bear—cried out to them bravely to do their duty, and defend the place, and pay no heed to her. But the men were not of that temper; they were at a loss; they feared Jensen, and this display of his daring unnerved them. They stood idly in a mass, while I, from where I stood, could see through the open door, to which no one else paid any heed, Jensen's men coming out of the wood, with only a few hundred yards of level ground between them and us. I was cumbered, as I told you, with some sea-coats, that I had caught up to make a couch for Mr. Ebrow, and as I held them to me with my left arm, they almost covered me from neck to knee. Now, in my pocket I carried the little pistol that Lancelot had given me, and in my first moment of surprise my right hand had involuntarily sought it out. Now, I was not much of a shot, and yet in a moment I made my mind up what I would do. I would, under cover of the coats, which I clutched to me, fire my piece through my pocket at Jensen, trusting to God to straighten the aim and guide the bullet. In that moment I took all the chances. If I hit Jensen, who was somewhat exposed to me where I stood, all would be well. If I missed him and he at once killed Marjorie, or if, missing him, I myself wounded or killed Marjorie, I knew that at least I should be doing as Marjorie would have me do, and in either of these cases we could despatch Jensen and have up our barricade again before help would come to him. All this takes time to tell, but took no time in the thinking, and my finger was upon the trigger when, in the providence of God, something happened which altered every purpose—Jensen's and the others', and mine. There came a great crash through the air loud as immediate thunder, with a noise that seemed to shake heaven above and earth below us. Every one of us in that narrow place knew it for the roar of a ship's gun.

140

CHAPTER XXXII

THE SEA GIVES UP ITS QUICK

The clatter of that reverberation altered in a trice the whole conditions of our game. Jensen, in his surprise, looked up for a moment, and in that moment I had flung myself upon him, and his pistol, going off, spent its bullet harmlessly in the skies. In another second he had knocked me to the ground with a force that nearly stunned me; but before he could use another weapon twenty hands were upon him, and twenty weapons would have ended him but for Lancelot's command to take him alive. In a trice we had flung our door in its place and swung the beam across, and there we were, none the worse for our adventure, with the chief of our enemies fast prisoner in our hands. Already the pirates were scouring back into the woods, and though certain of our men had the presence of mind to empty their muskets after them, and bring down the two rogues who had carried the sham Ebrow to us, most of us were occupied in peering through the loopholes on the other side of the fortress at a blessed sight. Not half a mile away rode the ship that had fired the shot; the smoke of the discharge was still in the air about her. She was a frigate, and she flew the Dutch flag.

You may imagine with what a rapture we saw that frigate and that flag. It could only mean succour, and we were sick at heart to think that we had no flag with us to fly in answer. But we waited and watched with beating hearts behind our walls, and presently we could see that a boat was lowered and that men came over the side and filled it, and then it began to make for Fair Island as fast as stroke of oar could carry it. With a cry of joy Lancelot thrust his spy-glass into my hand, crying out to me that Captain Amber was on board the boat. And so indeed he was, for I had no sooner clapped the glass to my eye than there I saw him, sitting in the stern in his brave blue coat, and at the sight of him my heart gave a great leap for joy. We opened our seaward gate at once, and in a moment Marjorie and Lancelot and I were racing to the strand, followed by half a dozen others, leaving the stockade well guarded, and orders to shoot Jensen on the first sign of any return of the pirates from the woods. Though, indeed, we felt pretty sure that they would make no further attempt against us, having lost their leader, and being now menaced by this new and unexpected peril.

As the boat drew nearer shore Lancelot tied a handkerchief to the point of his cutlass and waved it in the air, and at sight of it the figure in blue in the stern raised his hat, and the men rowing, seeing him do this, raised a lusty cheer, and pulled with a warmer will than ever, so that in a few more minutes their keel grated on the sand.

Captain Amber leaped out of the boat like a boy, splashing through the water to join us, while the Dutch seamen hauled the boat up and stared at us stolidly. Captain Amber clasped Marjorie's hand and murmured to himself 'Thank God!' while tears stood in his china-blue eyes, and were answered, for the first time that I ever saw them there, by tears in Marjorie's. Next he embraced Lancelot, and then he turned to me and wrung my hand with the same heartiness as on that first day in Sendennis, and it seemed to me for the moment as if that strand and island and all those leagues of land and water had ceased to be, and I were back again in the windy High Street, with my mother's shop-bell tinkling.

Only for a moment, however. There was no time for day-dreams. Hurriedly we told Captain Amber all that we had to tell. Much of the ugly story we found that he knew, and how he knew you shall learn later. Our immediate duty was to secure the pirates who were still at large on the island, and this proved an easy business. For the Dutch commander, who claimed the authority of his nation for all that region, sent one of his men with a flag of truce, accompanied by one of us for interpreter, to let them know that if they did not surrender unconditionally he would first bombard the wood in which they sheltered, and then land a party of men, who would cut down any survivors without mercy. As there was no help for it, the pirates did surrender. They came out of the woods, a sorry gang, and laid down their arms, and with the help of the Dutchmen, who lent us irons, we soon had the whole band manacled and helpless.

So there was an end of this most nefarious mutiny. With Cornelys Jensen fast in fetters the heart of the business would have been broken even without help from the sea. There was no man of all the others who was at all his peer, either for villainy or for enterprise and daring. Even if there had been, the pirates would have had no great chance, while, as it was, their case had no hope in it, and they succumbed to their fate in a kind of sullen apathy. Honest men had triumphed over rogues once more in the swing of the world's story, as I am heartily glad to believe that in the long run they always have done and always will do, until the day when rogues and righteous meet for the last time.

We soon heard of all that had happened to Captain Marmaduke after he left the Royal Christopher—or rather, after he had been forced to put forth from Early Island. It had been Captain Marmaduke's intention to make for Batavia, in the certainty of finding ships and succour there. By the good fortune of the fair weather, his course, if slow by reason of the little wind, was untroubled; and by happy chance, ere he had come to the end, he sighted the Dutch frigate, and spoke her. The Dutch captain consented to carry Captain Amber back to the wreck. On their arrival at Early Island they found the place in the possession of a few half-drunken mutineers, who were soon overpowered, and they learnt the tale of Jensen's treachery from the lips of the captive women. It was then that they sailed for Fair Island, with the women and prisoners on board, and arrived just in time to serve us the best turn in the world.

There was nothing for us now to do but to ship off our prisoners to Batavia in the frigate, where they would be dealt with by Dutch justice, and be hanged with all decorum, in accordance with the laws of civilised States. We were to go with the frigate ourselves, for at Batavia it was our Captain's resolve to buy him a new ship and so turn home to his own people and his own country, and try his hand no more at colonies, which was indeed the wisest thing he could do. Let me say here that to our great satisfaction we found Mr. Ebrow in the woods, tied nearly naked to a tree, alive and well, if very weak; but without a complaint on his lips or in his heart.

I was one of the earliest to go aboard the frigate, and the first sight I saw on her decks was a group of women huddled together in all the seeming of despair. These were the victims of the pirates' lust, and as they sat together they would wail now and then in a way that was pitiful to hear. But there was one woman who sat a little apart from the others and held her head high, and this woman was Barbara Hatchett. I scarce knew if I should approach her or no, but when she saw me, which was the moment I came aboard, she made me a sign with her head, and I at once went up to her. All the warm colour had gone out of her dark face, and the fire had faded from her dark eyes, but she was still very beautiful in her misery, and she carried herself grandly, like a ruined queen. As I looked at her my mind went back to that first day I ever saw her and was bewitched by her, and then to that other day when I found her in the sea-fellow's arms and thought the way of the world was ended. And for the sake of my old love and my old sorrow my heart was racked for her, and I could have cried as I had cried that day upon the downs. But there were no tears in the woman's eyes, and as I came she stood up and held out her hand to me with an air of pride; and I am glad to think that I had the grace to kiss it and to kneel as I kissed it.

'Well, Ralph,' she said, 'this is a queer meeting for old friends and old flames. We did not think of this in the days when we watched the sea and waited for my ship.'

I could say nothing, but she went on, and her voice was quite steady:

'This is a grand ship, but it is not my ship. My ship came in and my ship went out, and the devil took it and my heart's desire and me.'

143

She was silent for a moment, and then she asked me what the boats were bringing from the island. I told her that they were conveying the prisoners aboard to be carried to trial at Batavia. She heard me with a changeless face, as she looked across the sea where the ship's boats were making their way to the ship, and after awhile she asked me if I thought that we were bound to forgive our enemies and those who had used us evilly.

I was at a loss what to answer, but I stammered out somewhat to the effect that such was our Christian duty. The words stuck a little in my throat, for I did not feel in a forgiving mood at that moment.

'So Mr. Ebrow tells us,' she went on softly. Mr. Ebrow had been sent on board at once, and had immediately devoted himself, sick and weak though he was, to ministrations among the unhappy women. 'So Mr. Ebrow says, and he is a good man, and ought to know best. Shall I forgive, Ralph, shall I forgive?'

There was to me something infinitely touching in the way in which she spoke to me, as if she felt she had a claim upon me—the claim that a sister might have upon a brother.

I told her that Mr. Ebrow, being a man of God, was a better guide and counsellor than I, but that forgiveness was a noble charity. Indeed, I was at a loss what to say, with my heart so wrung.

'Well, well,' she said, 'let us forgive and forget,' and—for there was no restraint upon the movements of the woman—she moved toward the side, where they were lifting the manacled prisoners on board. Jensen was in the first batch, but not the first to be brought on board, and he carried himself sullenly, with his eyes cast down, and seemed to notice nothing as he was brought up on the deck. The prisoners were so securely bound that no especial guard was placed over them during the process of taking them from the boats, and so, before I was aware of it, Barbara had slipped by me and between the Dutch sailors, and was by Jensen's side. For the moment I thought that she had come to carry out her promise of forgiveness; but Jensen lifted his face, and I saw it, and saw that it was writhed with a great horror and a great fear. And then I saw her lift her hand, and saw a knife in her hand, and the next moment she had driven it once and twice into his breast by the heart, and Jensen dropped like a log, and his blood ran over the deck. Then she turned to me, and her face was as red as fire, and she cried out, 'Forgive and forget!' and so drove the knife into her own body and fell in her turn. It was all done so swiftly that there was no time for anyone to lift a hand to interfere, and when we came to lift them up they were both dead. This was the end of that beautiful woman, and this the end of Cornelys Jensen. He should have lived to be hanged; it was too good a death for him to die by her hand; but I can understand how it seemed to her hot blood and her wronged womanhood that

144

she could only wash out her shame by shedding her wronger's blood. May Heaven have mercy upon her!

CHAPTER XXXIII

THE LAST OF THE SHIP

It was many a weary month before we saw Sendennis again, but we did see it again. For Captain Marmaduke was so dashed by the untoward results of his benevolence and the failure of his scheme that he saw nothing better to do than to turn homeward, after mending his fortunes by the sale of the greater part of his Dutch plantations. A portion, however, he set apart and made over as a settlement for the remnant of the colonists, who, having got so far, had no mind to turn back, and as an asylum for the wretched women. With the aid of the Dutchmen we got the Royal Christopher off her reef and made shift to tow her into harbourage at Batavia, and there Captain Amber sold her and bought another vessel, wherein we made the best of our way back to England, with no further adventures to speak of. At Sendennis I had the joy to find my mother alive and well, and the wonder to find that my birth-place seemed to have grown smaller in my absence, but was otherwise unchanged.

And at Sendennis the best thing happened to me that can happen to any man in the world. For one morning, soon after our home-coming, I prayed Marjorie to walk with me a little ways, and she consented, and we went together outside the town and into the free sweet country. We fared till we came to that place where Lancelot once had found me, drowned in folly, and there I showed Marjorie the picture that Lancelot had given me, the picture of her younger self. And somehow as she took it from my hands and looked at it there came a little tremor to her lips and my soul found words for me to speak. I told her again that I loved her, that I should love her to the end of my days. I do not remember all I said; I dare say my words would show blunderingly enough on plain paper, but she listened to them quietly, looking at the sea with steady eyes. When I had done she stood still for a little, and then answered, and I remember every word she said.

'We are young, you and I, but I do not believe we are changeable. I feel very sure that you have spoken the truth to me; be very sure that I am speaking the truth to you. I love you!'

And so for the first time our lips met and the glory came into my life. I sailed the seas and made my fortune and married my heart's desire, and we roved the world together year after year, and always the glory staying with me in all its morning brightness.

All my life long I have hated parting from friends, parting from familiar faces and familiar places. Yet by the course which it has pleased Providence to give to my life it has been my lot to have many partings, both with well-loved men and women and with well-loved lands and dwellings. It is the plague of the wandering life, pleasant as it is in so many things, that it does of necessity mean the clasping of so many hands in parting, that it does of necessity mean the saying of so many farewells. Yet, after all, parting is the penalty of man for his transgression, and the most stay-at-home, lie-by-the-fire fellow has his share with the rest. Thus the philosopher by temperament, like my Lord Chesterfield, takes his friendships and even his loves upon an easy covenant, and the religious accept in resignation, and the rest shift as best they can. And so I hold out my hand and wish you good luck and God-speed!

THE END

CPSIA information can be obtained
at www.ICGtesting.com
Printed in the USA
LVHW110059010920
664725LV00011B/787

9 783752 436565